The High Wire

William Haggard has also written:

SLOW BURNER

THE TELEMANN TOUCH

VENETIAN BLIND

CLOSED CIRCUIT

THE ARENA

THE UNQUIET SLEEP

William Haggard
The High Wire

IVES WASHBURN, INC.
NEW YORK

THE HIGH WIRE

S   c.3

JAN 1 1 '68

BL

For
BLANCHE LUCAS

The High Wire

A tale of espionage involving British
security officers with a climax in
a stalled cable car high over the
Alps.

CHAPTER I

Sir William Banner was a successful industrialist and he was going to bed early. This he did not because his doctor had advised it, far less because he wasn't feeling well, but because bed was something he looked forward to. Sir William was asleep by eleven o'clock on every evening he could contrive it, and he slept eight and a half hours like a baby. He was sixty-five but didn't look it.

He climbed into his bath, lighting what he saw must be the last cigarette of the day. He rationed himself, but not too severely, and if he had felt like breaking the twenty-five he would have done so without troubling to excuse himself. He was an eminent industrialist but a very unpompous man.

He was humming a sad little tune which a listener might have misunderstood. For Sir William was in excellent heart. He had, he told himself, very good reason to be so. His firm had Project A— his consortium really, but it was a pretentious word and he didn't like it. A very important person had finally given him Project A a week ago. There had been negotiations whilst Maldington was being built, and Sir William Banner had considered them unnecessarily protracted. At bottom it had always been between himself and that fat ass Westerham, and Westerham hadn't got it. Now he, Bill Banner, had. It was as simple as that.

There was money in Project A and something else. He wouldn't for the moment think about the something else.

1

Instead he began to think about Rex Hadley. Sir William liked money and, within civilized limits, power; but best of all he liked a sense of purpose, the occasional casual evidence, flatly against the rest of it, that life wasn't wholly meaningless. For once or twice a year perhaps a piece dropped neatly in, and to Sir William Banner that was acutest pleasure.

Rex Hadley, for instance—he was getting a break at last. Poor bastard, he had had it thin. Sir William stretched in his bath, letting the warmth consume him. Rex Hadley and that awful wife. Irene— What a dreadful name! And what a dreadful woman. She'd been clever no doubt, something called intellectual, but the sharp chip she carried, the compulsion to be different, had hobbled Rex brutally. If there wasn't a prick to kick against Irene would seek one. Lost causes exhausted, Irene herself was lost. Not that she hadn't been fertile in invention. That ridiculous tribe in where was it? which somebody was supposed to be destroying. . . .

Sir William chuckled, for he'd had the best of that one. He'd agreed with her at once. He hadn't the least idea what she had been talking about but he'd agreed with her warmly at once. Her face had dropped a foot.

Naturally she had held Rex back. Rex Hadley was a first-class production engineer, and that wasn't something so easy to find. A good one, really good, should have been on the Board five years ago. But not with that wife. Sir William snorted, remembering that there were corporations—over-earnest he considered them— which treated wives very seriously indeed; he had heard that they even ran courses for them. Well, if they wanted to waste easy money, let them. To Sir William it was simpler: Rex Hadley had dragged a ball and chain, one wholly private. It wasn't for his employer to do anything to cut it.

But just the same, that visitor. . . . He had been a European contact man with a contract in his pocket which was well worth having. Entertainment had been arranged, a very good dinner as its climax. There had been a hint of final formality, for the Lady Banner of that

2

moment had been an admirable hostess. There had been wonderful food and wine, three hand-picked women, Lady Banner aside. Or rather there should have been, for one had been prevented and Irene had stood in. The notice had been minimal and Lady Banner desperate. But she hadn't been stupid. She had seated Irene where she couldn't engage the guest of honour short of shouting across the table. But afterwards, in the drawing-room, Lady Banner had been helpless.

It had been Africa, inevitably—a diatribe about something called colonialism. The guest had been surprised, then carefully non-committal. Irene had grated on, angry and hideously articulate. He had turned icily polite, finally contemptuous. Irene had been radiant. She'd made her preposterous point, fulfilled herself; she hadn't compromised.

The contract had gone to that fat ass Westerham.

Sir William began to dry himself. He liked Rex Hadley and respected him. He himself had had more than one wife, but he also had money, and money had meant that an intolerable situation could be ended with dignity. Moreover, he had no children, whereas Hadley had children and not much money. He'd made a mistake— you could see she looked down on him—but he'd stuck it till the children were afloat. That might be old fashioned but it wasn't despicable. How old was Rex Hadley now? Forty-five? But that was the prime of life. He wasn't bad-looking either—a medium figure, male. Women would look twice at him and not the Irene Hadleys. There were the years which the locusts had eaten but there was time to repair them still.

Sir William began to laugh. He had a high laugh, almost a giggle, something quite unexpected. But it made people smile and that was an asset. Sir William knew an asset when he saw one.

Rex Hadley again—there was an asset at last. Sir William had decided to give him Project A the moment he'd heard of the divorce. The decree absolute would take a month or two, but there wouldn't be any trouble. He supposed it was some put-up job, something some judge would tolerate. Just so long as the legal forms were decently observed in what he must realize was a public indecency. And there had been something about Irene's mother too: she'd been mean as hell and that hadn't helped, but now she was dead and she hadn't died penniless. Divorce wouldn't cripple Rex. Besides, he'd have good money now, for Project A was the sort of job worth it.

Six thousand—seven? He'd talk to his fellow directors. And if Project A came off there'd be a seat on the Board quite soon.

Sir William Banner slipped into bed. At the moment it was a single bed, and at sixty-five it was his intention that it should remain so. Sleep stalked him swiftly. . . . It had been a gratifying week: Project A was in his pocket and he'd given it to Rex Hadley. A good man held down, now up again. There was a pattern sometimes, something almost meaningful. Rex Hadley, forty-five. . . .

Banner envied Rex Hadley but he was happy for him too. He was a successful industrialist but a very nice man. He grunted, stretching opulently.

His housekeeper called him next morning at half-past seven. He hadn't stirred meanwhile.

With the hour's difference in Continental time Rex Hadley in Sestriere woke at half-past seven too. He had an arrangement with the hall porter to call him by telephone, and the instrument by his bedside had just done so with the discreet insistence appropriate to a hotel of the Conte's standing.

'Good morning, sir. There was fresh snow in the night.'

'Good news. And thank you.'

Rex Hadley put down the receiver, choosing a bellpush from three on a panel. Over each was a little figure—chambermaid, boots and floor-waiter. Rex rang for the floor-waiter, thinking that the term was formally a misnomer since at the Conte there were no floors. It was built around a fascinating spiral. While he waited he walked

4

to the window. There had been four inches at least, a layer of powder snow on crisp old crust. In those conditions it was possible to persuade yourself that you could really ski.

The waiter came in quietly. He had coffee and milk on a tray, and two fresh pears, for he had been bringing Rex his breakfast for three days. He put the tray on a table, waving at the snow outside. 'Sestriere,' he said dramatically, 'is saved.'

'Oh, I don't know. It wasn't really dangerous yet.'

'Not for fine skiers.' The waiter bowed. He knew perfectly well that Rex Hadley wasn't a fine skier but barely competent, since at the Conte your class in the snow was something known at once. But he was a courteous man and an excellent waiter. 'Not for good skiers,' he said again, 'but for the rest. . . .' His shrug dismissed the rest. 'Two broken legs, both foreigners.'

It was evident it didn't distress him.

Rex Hadley poured the coffee.

'Attention lest it scald.' The waiter bowed again and left.

Rex shaved quickly with a razor Sir William had given him. Now there was a good one to work for. There were chairmen who would have made a song and dance; looked serious; boomed. Sir Bill had been almost casual. He'd told him about Project A and Maldington, and Rex had caught his breath; then he'd tossed him the job of running it. . . . His salary? Sir Bill hadn't spoken to his Board yet, but it wouldn't be less than twice what Rex was getting. When did he start? Well, he didn't—not yet. For a moment Sir William had been as near to solemn as he allowed himself. Rex mustn't suppose that the head of a firm was wholly ignorant about his senior staff. Rex was—well, Rex had been under strain, and it wasn't sensible to start on an important job bang following a time of strain. Sir William lit one of the twenty-five, counting the others, nodding contentedly. So Rex must have a fortnight at least. Unfortunately he couldn't have a fortnight—not right off. But he could have a week, he *must* have a week, and then, when Maldington was ticking over—call it a fortnight more—he could go on the rest

5

of it. Hadn't he once been keen on wintersports? (Sir William had said snowballing.) Then that was the best bet in the middle of the winter. There'd be exercise at least, sun with a bit of luck, and always a change of food. Sir William had a simple faith in change of food. And he'd been making some inquiries. There wasn't much snow in Switzerland ('Which is excellent news. I loathe the Swiss') but there was plenty at Sestriere. A first class hotel as well. The Conte. Sir William had stayed there.

He had risen decidedly. So that was all fixed. I'll see you in ten days or so. And by the way, there's five hundred in your bank account. Advance on the extra, you know. Goodbye for now. Enjoy yourself.

Rex Hadley went out into the cold clear air, conscious that he had lungs and that here at least they functioned. He went down to the ski school and put on his skis, looking at the soft fresh snow, considering a decision. So far he'd been cautious, for he hadn't ski-ed since boyhood—quick trips, travelling hard and living even harder; he'd been taking the easiest slopes, climbing again to the modest start by a ski-lift called Baby. He'd fallen but never seriously, and confidence was returning. Today he'd try a medium run. There was a chairlift back in case he came to grief on it.

He spent a day of increasing bliss, lunching in a bar at the bottom of the piste off salame and an unlikely salad. When it was dark he left, leaving his skis at the school, walking back to the Conte. He was stiff but not tired, which pleased him, for at first he had been exhausted. He took a bath and read for a while in the admirably heated bedroom, relishing the warmth. Irene had had the passion of her class for open windows at all times, but Continentals saw no virtue in cold bedrooms. He brushed his hair, still black, and a firm square face looked back at him. His skin, he saw, looked a good deal fresher. Then he went down to the bar.

He hadn't used it before since he hadn't been in the mood for it, but now he looked around him, enjoying the casual intimacy. There was a brisk little band and three or four couples dancing. The

6

girls wore their trousers still and for once had the figures for them; the men had hairy sweaters of impossible design or, the sophisticates these, utterly plain ones. After dinner it would be a little more formal. There were one or two couples at tables, not dancing.

Rex walked to the bar, ordering Aperol. He was thinking that when nobody else was ordering spirits, then nor did you wish to. Not that he was a drinker anyway. There had been times in the last ten years when the bottle had seriously tempted. A native stubbornness had saved him. Drink wasn't an escape but only a palliative. If he waited. . . .

Well, he'd waited.

He moved his shoulders unconsciously, shifting a past burden, ordering another Aperol. A man from one of the tables had crossed to the bar, ordering for himself, and as Rex lifted his drink the man moved unexpectedly. He seemed to have lost his balance, tripping against an empty stool. He fell against Rex and the drinks went over.

'I'm extremely sorry. I was terribly clumsy.' The English was perfect but it wasn't quite an Englishman's.

'Not at all.'

The stranger looked at Rex's glass. There was a quarter of an inch of dark pink fluid still, and the stranger observed it. He didn't hesitate, nor fuss; he turned to the barman.

'An Aperol, please, and two Camparis.' The barman was mopping up. 'And serve the Aperol first. One Campari is for my table. One.' There were two people at it. 'The other I'll drink here.'

'You're very kind,' Rex said.

'And possibly presumptuous.' The distinguished-looking stranger smiled. 'I've lived in England and I know that one doesn't introduce oneself. It's the sin against the Holy Ghost. Just the same, this isn't England. It's a resort and an international one.' He considered Rex Hadley, entirely serious. 'I'll risk it,' he said finally. 'I'll risk a snub. My name's de Fleury.'

'And mine's Rex Hadley.'

7

'Indeed?' de Fleury considered Rex again, at last said carefully: 'I remember a Mrs. Rex Hadley. I met her once at dinner. That was some years ago. I was working in armaments then.'

' We've just divorced.'

'Ah, so?'

It was exquisitely done. 'Ah, so?' was what he said, but he conveyed a great deal more. He suggested a certain sympathy, almost an approval. It was certain that both were men. One needn't talk.

de Fleury raised his glass. 'Your very good health.'

'And yours.'

'You're alone here?'

'Yes.'

'I'm with the lady at my table.' de Fleury nodded across the room. 'The man I do not know. He is English but he introduced himself. So he cannot be wholly English.' de Fleury finished his drink, staring across it at his table. 'Come to that he doesn't quite look it. I suppose you wouldn't care to join us?'

'Of course. With pleasure.'

'In that case I'll buy him a drink. He sat down at my table and I didn't invite him. You will have gathered that the lady isn't Madame de Fleury. That is mitigated by the fact that there isn't one, but informality has its limits still. But since there are four of us. . . .' de Fleury beckoned to the barman. 'A bottle to my table, please. The one we had last night. The Heidsieck 'fifty-two.'

They walked to de Fleury's table and he made the introductions: 'Miss Francom.'

Rex bowed.

'And Mr.—er, Mr. . . .'

The other had stood up. 'Julian Cohn,' he said.

'Ah, yes, of course.'

It had been beautifully done again, but this time it had grated. Rex was certain de Fleury had known Cohn's name; he'd caught it the first time when Cohn had introduced himself, and he hadn't forgotten. It had been a tiny insult but precisely calculated.

8

Rex sat down beside Miss Francom. He put her at thirty plus, though the plus defeated him. She had a fine full figure and competent hands, the high cheekbones of the mid-European. There were the smooth dark hair he liked, humour in the clear grey eyes, and the air that whatever her years were they hadn't been empty. You wouldn't have called her pretty but there were other, maturer words. Her English, like de Fleury's, was almost perfect. She said promptly: 'Just for the record I'm Mary Francom. I don't know how I acquired the Mary, and Francom isn't my real name either. But it's near enough to the original for the English to get their tongues round.'

'You've lived in England long?'

'Five or six years. Since the trouble in my country.'

'You speak wonderful English.'

She laughed. 'Of course I do—we're a race of linguists. We have to be. I speak German and French besides my own language. I can even get on in Serbo-Croat.'

'I envy you. I'm very bad at languages.'

'I wouldn't let it worry you, your own is international.'

'But it makes me feel pretty insular. You had three or four languages anyway, and now you've added English. I suppose that was in England.'

'Not quite. I had a bit of grounding—my father insisted on it. In my country English wasn't a necessity like the others but a'— she waved a handsome hand—'a sort of class indicator.'

He laughed in turn; he was finding it extraordinarily easy to talk to Mary Francom. 'So you're a romantic middle-Europe aristocrat.'

'Not on your life. My father was a tradesman, a successful one. That's what got him into trouble. He had two shops, one on each side of the river. They shot him,' she said coolly, 'he was lucky.'

'I'm sorry if I've been stupid.'

'No. It was six years ago and I don't do too badly. I'm a nurse.'

It surprised him. The hands, he thought, the air of competence. But de Fleury, the Conte, the beautiful fur across the chairback. . . .

9

It was none of his business.

The champagne had come to the table and the waiter was pouring it. Julian Cohn was rather quiet. He had small sharp eyes and he moved them constantly. He wasn't a talker but not much missed him. de Fleury didn't try to engage him; he turned easily to Rex.

'You've been here before, I expect?'

'No, never. As it happens I haven't ski-ed since I was a boy. I've been taking it pretty easy but today I tried Piste Nine.'

'I saw you. I think you're too modest. I'm not at all good myself.'

Cohn said unexpectedly: 'He's quite first class.'

It might almost have been a warning.

'Nonsense. In any case I don't come here purely to ski. Serious ski-ing is too much like work, and it's a wonderful place to relax.'

'I'm doing that too.'

'Indeed?' de Fleury smiled. 'You have the air,' he said.

'I don't know how you spotted it. I didn't choose to come. My chairman sent me.'

'Sensible chairman.'

'He's a very shrewd man. I start a new job next week.'

de Fleury made a half bow. 'An important one, naturally.'

'Yes, it's important.' Rex hadn't meant to say it but he had. And after all, why not? Project A was important and to spare. He'd merely confirmed a statement.

de Fleury beckoned to the waiter, saying something quickly in Italian. Another bottle arrived smoothly and de Fleury poured it himself. Julian Cohn declined and Rex said deprecatorily: 'I'm not much of a drinker.'

'Drinker? Two glasses of champagne?'

'I haven't drunk champagne for years.'

'The better to enjoy it now.'

The band had stopped and the room was emptying. Rex noticed that his glass had been refilled. He drank it as a courtesy and rose. He was astonished to discover that he wasn't quite steady. It was nothing, he told himself—just a hand on the back of his chair.

Nevertheless it had been true: he wasn't a drinking man. Four glasses of champagne on an empty stomach, two unaccustomed shorts before them. Not that there was much in Aperol. Just the same. . . .

He said firmly: 'It's been delightful. Now I must go and change.'

de Fleury seemed almost shocked. 'But you can't break up the evening. The band will be back in an hour, and dinner's nothing wonderful. It's eatable but it's international food. Look, I've taken a little liberty again. I spoke to the waiter just now. An omelette, I thought, if that would suit you, and afterwards cheese if we want it. We needn't leave this table.'

Rex hesitated, standing. He hadn't been telling the truth, or not quite all of it. He had spoken of changing but he hadn't been thinking of dinner; he'd been thinking of lying down. An aspirin perhaps. . . . Finally he shrugged. de Fleury at least had been accurate. Rex Hadley was on holiday. He knew that he'd earned one.

He sat down determinedly.

It was a remarkably pleasant evening. Rex danced with Mary Francom. She danced very well, light and strong, and he held her with pleasure, watching her wide smile. At something around eleven she had left them, but Julian Cohn sat on. His presence had been the evening's only flaw, for it was obvious that he annoyed de Fleury. de Fleury had tried to shed him; in his worldly way he had even been gently rude. Rex had thought it curious. Cohn didn't look insensitive, and clearly he wasn't wanted, but he had sat on stolidly, his bright eyes moving. Always he listened. Rex had talked easily, aware that he was talking well. de Fleury had been interested, charming. There had been more champagne.

They had gone to bed at a little past midnight. Rex, waking at dawn with a headache he wasn't accustomed to, could remember it perfectly, since it was something he had been obliged to give thought to. He hadn't been drunk but he had taken wine. He could walk—but with forethought. Once moving it had been wise to move: no sudden stops, no turns. The porter had worked the lift for him.

He forced himself out of bed, finding the aspirin, drinking a pint of water. He was feeling a malaise which wasn't purely physical, knowing it for a sense of shame, a small shame, but nagging. It wouldn't let him sleep again, and Rex took his dressing-gown.

. . . But it was humiliatingly simple: he'd talked too much and about himself. He hadn't exactly boasted but he'd felt a need to justify. He'd met three strangers, two of them charming, the sort of people he hadn't met for years. So he'd talked about his important work, implying his own importance. Despicable, of course: no doubt there were frightful words for it.

Rex Hadley grunted. He didn't blame the drink—he was much too intelligent. Drink released tensions not secrets, something in the man himself. Besides, he had little to hide still. Project A wasn't one of those melodramatic secrets which you could reduce to some formula; steal; microfilm to Moscow. It was what its name called it, a project. It wasn't impossible that nothing would emerge from it.

He grunted again. The fact remained that he'd been indiscreet. Ten years he'd lost—held back and frustrated. He'd escaped in the end but the wounds were too recent. He'd wanted reassurance, balm. He'd fished for it, and when it came he'd gobbled it.

He decided he'd learnt a lesson, one mercifully timed. Had it happened three months later, when he'd been in charge at Malding-ton, perhaps when they'd really got the thing. . . .

He might have dropped something vital. He had once met a Colonel Russell, something big in the Security Executive, and Russell's talk had fascinated him. He'd been talking about screening people, not its techniques but its basic principles. For instance, a man with a disreputable mistress, even one suspect, wasn't neces-sarily a bad risk provided he was living happily with her. . . . That surprised Mr. Hadley? It was apt to surprise most people, but its roots were in sound psychology. A man could be unconventional, even dissolute, and still stay perfectly secure. The man who was dangerous was the man who had something to hide. Not his secret, but about himself. *Inside* himself. Psychiatrists had their own mumbo-jumbo, words of six syllables. Russell hadn't thought much of them. He had another and simpler. He looked for a happy man. The happy man kept secrets.

Rex Hadley sent for coffee. Very well, he'd be happy. He'd learnt a cheap lesson and he meant to remember. He wouldn't avoid de Fleury: that would look odd. de Fleury was an expert skier, the sort of rich playboy you met at the Conte. With girl friend in tow. Except that she'd been extremely nice. No, he wouldn't avoid de Fleury. If it came to pushing his psyche around he knew that he didn't want to.

The room was very hot, even for a nation which detested to be cold. The furniture was public property, grand and very ugly. The heat had long since spoiled the marqueterie.

A middle-aged man sat in it, expectant, not yet smoking; he was awaiting his master, and his master had a formidable opinion of his own importance. The middle-aged man called himself Victor, and his surname was never used. He wore his hair *en brosse* and his face had the stamp of arms. And something as well, an utter dedication. It was an intelligent face but frightening.

Presently the Marshal came in. He was a tall man with a belly which a weakness for wearing uniform did nothing to conceal. Once, twenty years ago, he had fought a small but classic tank action; thereafter he had earned a solid reputation as an international nuisance; now he was Messiah.

Or recently he had been: now he was slipping and knew it. They shook hands formally and both men sat down. Speaking his language a trifle too precisely the tall man said: 'The balance of power in Europe. . . . We've got to have this English thing, we've got to have it too.'

'My Marshal, it will be difficult. After all, they're our nominal

13

allies.' Victor was putting the difficulties, doing his duty. It was his unspoken opinion that the tall man was half a mystic. And mystics were hell. Talk to one sensibly, nail him on an evident *non sequitur*, and promptly he slipped away from you.

But the tall man was staring at him. 'Victor,' he said, 'dear Victor.' They had been at military school together, a dozen stricken fields, a hundred beds. Sickening defeats on one, too easy victories to compensate.

Victor didn't answer.

The tall man was suddenly furious. He rose to his considerable height, talking with dreadful fluency. Country, he said, and honour. The motherland. Glory.

He sat down at last. . . . Somewhere—in London possibly but much more likely Washington—was the most secret of all secret rooms. It would be heavily guarded, by men and by the latest inventions of Anglo-Saxon devilry. The Anglo-Saxons met in it in crisis; they discussed and they bargained; finally they decided, but they never consulted the tall man. On the contrary, in any dilemma they blandly betrayed his interests. Moreover they hogged things, never sharing information on what was established, far less on anything new. And this was new indeed.

Victor sighed quietly. He was head of the special service, a practical man with the fears of his type and training. What he feared most was obsession, the tall man's in particular. The Marshal's obsession was that his country was still a Power.

Victor wasn't obsessive but he was something more effective. He was the Army or an influential part of it.

But the tall man had risen suddenly, stalking from the room. It was his opinion that he had decided something. Victor lit a black cheroot. Far to the East he had lost an arm, but he'd acquired the habit of the black cheroot. Country, he thought, and honour. The motherland. Glory.

Oh God, not that again.

He took a staff car back to his modest office. In it he re-read a

14

telegram. It was a serious telegram—much too serious to show the Marshal. Victor had simply suppressed it. Decoded it read simply.

FIRST CONTACT MADE AS INSTRUCTED. HAS TALKED ONLY IN GENERAL TERMS BUT HAS USED THE PHRASE PROJECT A WHICH IS CLEARLY IMPORTANT, PROBABLY THE SAME ALREADY REPORTED TO US. CONTACT RETURNS TO ENGLAND SUNDAY AS EXECUTIVE HEAD OF PROJECT A. AM FOLLOWING. SEND SOONEST BACKGROUND ENGLISHMAN JULIAN COHN, JOURNALIST, CRYPTO.

Victor began to write an answer. Coded it would go to a little town in Piedmont. There a waiter would decode it and take out a tiny car. He'd drive to Sestriere and he'd know where to find de Fleury. Colonel de Fleury he called himself.

Not that he'd always been one.

CHAPTER II

Major Robert Mortimer of the Security Executive was to lunch with Miss Francom in a quarter of an hour, and it was an appointment he was looking forward to. She was a woman he admired, and not only because she was one of his six best agents.

He was a man of something over forty, tall and very neat; he looked what he was, the ex-Regular officer. He owed his job to a combination of unblushing nepotism and a judgement of himself which had been quite detached; and, as often infuriatingly happened when it would have been easy to predict failure, maliciously to hope for it, he did his work excellently. His master was Colonel Charles Russell, the head of the Executive—bland, indestructible and cool. Russell had served with his father. Mortimer himself had been in a regiment which after the war had been amalgamated with another. The shotgun marriage had been resented, and the wife had the reputation that she successfully advanced herself. Robert Mortimer, a Regular, had known what that meant: he was a major and would stay so. He sent in his papers and went to Charles Russell.

Russell had asked him to stay the weekend. He had golfed with him; talked trivialities; watched how he drank and when. He had motored him back to London on the Monday, still saying nothing.

Four days later Mortimer had been invited to join the Security Executive. Now he was an Assistant Director, one of three. He knew he was in line when Russell went. Not that the thought excited him. He wasn't insanely ambitious and he adored Charles Russell.

He rose, glancing in the mirror, since he wasn't a man to lunch with a lady dirty. . . . A sober suit and spotless shirt, a City-ish sort of tie. He never wore his regiment's, an affair of appalling stripes. His shoes, he saw, would have passed his batman.

His turn-out would do.

He was taking Mary Francom to a Grill and Cheese, and for various reasons variously calculated. To begin with he liked meat, and he knew where the meat was good. To continue he wasn't rich, and a great many people knew him. His work was known but Mary's wasn't: it would have been foolish to risk notice somewhere flash, but lunch with an attractive woman at a Grill and Cheese would hardly suggest a principal and agent. He knew she wouldn't wear her treasured fur. It was far too grand for an honest nurse.

In his taxi he smiled. It was marvellous cover, that nursing home.

He walked into the grill room, seeing that she was already seated. She wasn't in furs but she didn't need them. And she was looking very well. As he sat down he saw that she had started.

'I was hungry,' she said simply. 'I began without you. Once you've been really hungry you never catch up on it. Never.'

He was looking at a plate of scampi. 'Don't spoil your steak.'

'I won't. I eat like a horse.'

'But you keep your figure.'

She looked at him, pleased. 'That's the first time you've ever noticed me. Me or my figure.'

'I'm noticing it now.'

'Keep looking,' she said.

He turned to the waitress, ordering quickly. 'Two large fillet steaks with mushrooms. Salad with French dressing. A carafe of red wine. The steak for the lady medium. I like my own well done.'

Miss Francom raised a well-kept eyebrow. When the waitress had gone she asked: 'What's this about well done?'

'I like my meat well done.'

'And I like honest men.'

'What's so honest?'

Miss Francom sighed. 'I eat with a lot of men, you know. Most of the time you're making me, and just occasionally I'm working for myself. So I eat with a lot of men and most of them order rare. They wouldn't at home.' She looked round the room. 'I estimate that half the steak in London is eaten on expense accounts. Which means that it's eaten *for* expense accounts. Which means that it's eaten to impress. Eat steak with a business contact and you order rare. It's the he-man thing to do.'

'I know what you mean. And the rest of your London steak?'

'Is eaten with women. Whom you want to impress again, though maybe for different reasons. So again you order rare. That makes you a he-man—you hope.'

'I'll order mine rare next time.'

She said coolly: 'You wouldn't need that.'

There was a comfortable little silence.

'You're pretty observant,' he said.

'I have to be. I've just been doing some observing. On your behalf and at your expense. You'll be getting a bill for the extras. We were at Sestriere.'

'That's what we're here to talk about.'

'My gallant Major Mortimer!' She dropped her voice but not extravagantly. 'I've been running with de Fleury for a month, ever since you told me what he was and asked me to cover him. It wasn't difficult to arrange, because he'd been to the nursing home. It was nothing severe, an impacted wisdom tooth, but I made it my business to nurse him personally.' She drank some wine reflectively. 'He's a spy and I don't much like him, but he's very generous. What he gives me and what you do. . . .' She looked up suddenly. 'One job,' she said, 'two salaries for doing it. I save. One day I'll be shot of all of you.'

'I'm not a moralist.'

'I know you're not. If you were I wouldn't be explaining things.'

'I know what you've been through.'

There was another little silence, then: 'Where were we, Bob?'

'At Sestriere.'

'Yes, with de Fleury. We came back four days ago.' She drank some more wine, declining fruit. 'Have you heard of a man called Hadley?'

'Indeed I have.'

'Have you heard of a Project A?'

'But you shouldn't even know the word.'

'I guessed it. This Hadley mentioned Project A. To Francis de Fleury.'

Robert Mortimer swore.

'But I doubt if it's that serious. Hadley wasn't technically secure but he wasn't stupid either. He mentioned Project A but he said nothing about it.'

'How did it happen?'

'Much as you might expect. de Fleury scraped acquaintance with Rex Hadley, then brought him to our table. He ordered a lot of champagne and Hadley drank it. I don't think he's a drinking man. I liked him. He mentioned this Project A.'

'You're sure there was nothing else?'

'How can I be? I wasn't ski-ing. They may have gone up in a cable-car and Hadley may have talked again. But I'd cheerfully bet against it.'

'Why?' Robert Mortimer had barked it.

'Don't snap my head off, Bob. I'm going on Hadley's manner— I'm a woman. Rex Hadley drank a bit and he talked pretty large, but next morning he was cagey. I don't know whether he remembered dropping an actual clanger but I'm certain he knew he'd talked too much.'

'He avoided de Fleury?'

'I told you he wasn't stupid. Besides, I was with de Fleury.'

'It went like that?'

'Why not? I like Rex Hadley a lot, and I wasn't being paid to watch him.'

She was dining with him that evening. That had nothing to do with the Security Executive.

'Then tell me the rest.'

'There wasn't much of it. de Fleury tried again but he got nowhere. I know nothing about this Project A except that it's clearly important. So, I should say, was Rex. Who'd been talking too much but realized it. It warned him, I think: he put himself on notice. He was polite but he wouldn't be drawn.'

'And that's the lot?'

'Except for a man called Julian Cohn.'

Mortimer said deliberately: 'Who is coming to see me this afternoon.'

'Then you know him too?'

'He says I do. He said we'd met at a house I've certainly been to, though I don't remember him. More important, we've a file on him.'

'It wouldn't surprise me. He told us he was a journalist and he told us the papers he writes for. He can't possibly live on that. He's written a book as well, something with a title like "Baldwin the Fascist Prototype". Very left, very militant. Arrogant too. I don't think it sold much.'

'And what did he do at Sestriere?'

'Nothing—that's the point. But he stuck to us like glue. He doesn't talk but he listens—goodness, he listens. de Fleury tried to shake him off but Cohn outfaced him.'

'Was he with you when Hadley mentioned Project A?'

'He was. My guess is that he noticed it. And why should he do that?'

'He's a journalist.'

'With very long ears, even for his trade. And there's another thing. There was a chambermaid, somebody in Victor's organization, I suppose. One day I came in suddenly and de Fleury was talking to her about Cohn. I didn't hear in detail but he was asking her to find out something about him.'

'Interesting,' Robert said.

'To you, perhaps.' Mary looked at her watch. 'Well, I've another job.'

He paid the bill and rose. On an impulse he asked her quickly: 'You wouldn't care to dine tonight? Pure pleasure for a change. Pleasure for me.'

'Ask me again, but I've a date tonight.'

They walked out into a bitter cold. It had been snowing, then freezing, and the traffic was in chaos. He found her a taxi and put her in, an elegant, ample, exciting woman.

He decided to walk, buying an evening paper, glancing at the headlines, turning to the Stop Press at the back. There was nothing that interested him and he started to fold the paper. Then he stopped suddenly, reading intently. It was a very small paragraph but he read it three times. There had been an accident in Wheatley Street and it looked like a hit-and-run. A man had been found unconscious and his injuries were serious.

The man had been taken to a near-by nursing home. He was a resident of Wheatley Street and his identity had been established.

Mr. Julian Cohn wouldn't be keeping his appointment.

CHAPTER III

Robert Mortimer went back to the Security Executive. He wrote a careful report for Colonel Russell on everything which had happened at Sestriere. The Executive knew all about Project A, or to be accurate its business was to ensure that nobody else knew anything. The Executive had its own men at Maldington, and a senior officer at headquarters, Robert Mortimer in fact, charged with co-ordination. It was a very vague word and an awkward duty, since Project A wasn't a secret but simply a possibility which the scientists of six nations must have scented. Robert Mortimer sighed. He knew about formal secrets and something of how to keep them (when, he remembered, an open society let him), but projects were different. What lay at the end of Project A was something which could change overnight the balance of power in Europe or, quite conceivably, it wasn't a weapon at all. But that was known widely, in other and rival Powers. The thing was on in theory, but it was going to need massive luck. And it seemed that the English had had it. The English were mad, but they didn't commit enormous resources to programmes of abstract science. That wasn't their form at all. So they must have had a breakthrough—small perhaps, nothing final—but enough to encourage them. Why otherwise build Maldington? Clearly it had cost millions, and it had sprung from a wasteland with a speed which suggested that in any case cost was irrelevant. It was supposed to be the latest in engineering shops but nobody believed

22

it. A board had gone up in the past ten days—'Sir William Banner and Partners'. Nobody believed that either. Sir William was an industrialist, and industrialists had experience, competitive know-how, which no government scientist had. So some physicist had stumbled on something, and Maldington had risen as his nameless monument. But Sir William had taken it over; Sir William could develop things, maybe produce and fast. The latest in engineering shops? Sophisticated eyebrows rose. That wire, dear boy, the dogs, the ex-sergeant majors absurdly disguised as doormen. It didn't look nuclear, so. . . .

Robert Mortimer frowned. He was technically ignorant of what went on at Maldington: his business was to keep the world so.

It wouldn't, he knew, be easy. The others must be on notice too, the others would want it. The English had got on to something— what? Five Powers it could affect and one it could relegate finally. That Power was de Fleury's.

Mortimer knew about de Fleury. He knew his private story and could guess his public aim. Major Mortimer took him seriously. It was fortunate Mary Francom was a woman.

Now he was sealing his report on what she'd brought him. He had told the facts simply, leaving judgement to Russell. Who would probably talk to Sir William Banner before deciding what to do about Rex Hadley. And as for Cohn, there were already papers. Mortimer had them himself since he wished to refresh his memory.

He began to read steadily. Mortimer had several dozen files which, with a change of name, would have done for Julian Cohn, and they had always troubled him. To begin with he didn't understand the men and women whose dossiers they were. Mary Francom had been right, for Cohn didn't live on journalism. His grandfather had owned a grocer's shop, his father a chain of them. It was a company now with a considerable capital, and Cohn still owned most of it. He was third generation, ripe for the higher thought, but he hadn't divested himself of the private fortune which his higher thought detested. He wrote for the left wing journals and he wrote very well, bitter little articles never quite scurrilous and never quite fair. Then he went home to a comfortable flat in Wheatley Street, paying the rent from a chain of successful grocers. Cohn was in the movement, very much so. Private fortunes were out of date—God, they were an outrage—but he went home to live on one, very cosily indeed. He was a part of a recognizable establishment, one smaller but just as definite as the other with a capital. Which he attacked incessantly. But he lived like his enemies, more so than most of them. It struck Robert Mortimer as odd. He wasn't a moralist, Mary Francom had said so, but he had a sensitive nose for hypocrisy.

That was the background and it was all too familiar. It was what came after which was interesting to the Executive. For Julian Cohn had contacts, *avant-garde* lecturers and economists, novelists who called themselves committed; and, since he had means to do so, Cohn had gone farther than this twilight world.

He had very close contact with an embassy. It wasn't de Fleury's. One thing at least was certain: Julian Cohn wouldn't have been working for de Fleury's masters.

Robert Mortimer looked at his engagement book. He had an hour to spare and he put on his hat; he found a taxi and told it to go to Wheatley Street. There he dismissed it.

He looked around him, interested. The street was a bylane of doctorland. There were maisonettes one side, a block of flats the other, and a pub whose customers he could have sketched unseen. The comfortable little street ran at right angles between two others, the stroke to a capital H. It wasn't wide and it had recently been metered. Mortimer looked around again, more interested than ever. He paced it out, seventy-five ex-Regular strides. He walked across, which was eight and a half. But on one side were continuous parking spaces, and all were still occupied. A few hours ago they would hardly have been clear, for this was a metered parking ground—doctors and dentists and a hospital round the corner. So take off two paces for a solid line of cars one side. Nor was the other clear. The metering wasn't continuous here but it was more than half the street again. So take off another two paces. What you were left with was an effective road space of at most twelve feet, twelve feet of driving space connecting a street which was hardly important with another almost as tatty. Seventy-five paces long, so you wouldn't have been belting it. Mortimer looked at Wheatley Street again. The snow had melted, frozen to an ugly ice. In a reliable car with first-class brakes he'd have been doing fifteen at best. It struck him as a very strange place to knock a man down.

Unless, of course, you'd meant to.

He walked thoughtfully to a telephone box, dialling a police station.

'Macdonald? Robert Mortimer here.'

'Good evening, sir. What can I do for you?'

'That accident of yours—the one in Wheatley Street.'

'Oh yes?' The polite West Highland voice was cagey.

'Nothing to do with us, of course. It's just that we knew the man. We'd an interest in Mr. Cohn.'

'Indeed, sir?' Macdonald was unexcited. An admirable policeman, he did police work admirably. He knew little about the Executive; he didn't want to. 'I can't tell you much for we simply don't know it. This Cohn seems to have walked into the roadway and some fool sends him flying, and perhaps lost his head and drove on. We've not found a soul who saw it, but we may.' There was a second's hesitation, then: 'There weren't any signs of brake-marks, but the road was ice.'

'Hadn't they cleared it?' Robert Mortimer hid a smile. He wasn't falling for that one; he wasn't disclosing that he'd been poking about in Wheatley Street.

Like a policeman, he thought. That was really a little naughty. He asked again: 'Hadn't they cleared it?'

'You don't know our Borough Council, sir.'

'I didn't know Cohn—not personally.'

'Most respectable citizen. Lived with a housekeeper. Most respectable too. A Scot.'

Robert said quickly: 'Of course.' He knew it was expected.

'He's pretty badly hurt, they say. He'll live or he won't.'

'Unconscious?'

'Very. And probably for days. They took him to a nursing home.' Macdonald named it.

'I'll just scribble the address down.' Robert Mortimer was indulging a mild deception. He wasn't scribbling the address down since it was one well known to him. 'Keep me in touch, if you would. I don't suppose there's anything, but Cohn was a customer. We like to keep the books straight.'

'Certainly, sir. Good night.'

Major Mortimer found another cab, driving south through a pompous street. A hundred yards down it he glanced at a familiar house. It was the nursing home named by the police. The road was stiff with nursing homes but this had been nearest to Wheatley Street.

Also it was Miss Francom's. Who would recognize Julian Cohn again. Who'd know what to report and where.

On Sunday evening Rex Hadley was driving back to his new little house at Maldington. It was a small red box, prefabricated, raised with astonishing speed, and very ugly. But it wasn't uncomfortable. A couple looked after him whom Rex had found waiting when he'd finally moved in. There had been a note from Sir William too. Sir William had interviewed the couple himself and Rex had Sir Bill's assurances: the man drove well and the woman's cooking wasn't poisonous.

Rex looked at Maldington in the light of an early moon, driving alongside the perimeter fence. The administrative block rose in the centre, stark and unlovely; the enormous cooling towers shone dully in the moonlight. There was a mass of gantries, and piping ran between building and building, incalculably, twisted in an almost human agony. Maldington was high science and looked it; it was a laboratory—a factory in name—but a laboratory conscious of destiny. Here a handful of men and women might tip the scales of policy, of power in Europe. Under the moon it was somehow sentient, a night beast stretching in its accustomed light, silently flexing its muscles.

Rex reined his fancies sharply, driving on. Now there were smaller buildings, carefully spaced, the upper part slotted planking varnished brown and bright new glass below. They were as modern as a shoe shop. All were within the perimeter fence, six feet of chain-wire or a little more, held upright on concrete posts. At the top the posts leant outwards, carrying on angle-bars what seemed to be barbed wire. Three strands were exactly that but the fourth was deceptive: if you looked closely there were insulators hidden in the stanchions carrying it; the current was turned on at night. Inside the fence were obstacles again, double and triple where it mattered. There were doors which opened as you approached them. Properly, that is. If you approached them wrongly they strangely stayed shut. There were matters you couldn't see, or feel, things which went bump in the night. At the heart, it was rumoured, was a good deal worse.

And as light relief there were always the notices. Rex was near one now and he read it appreciatively:

DOGS PATROL THIS ESTABLISHMENT AT NIGHT

He grinned, for the rubric tickled a cool humour. Patrol—that was excellent. It had something military but something domestic too. Patrolling dogs—dear me, they must be most intelligent. And what it might have said but didn't: Savage Hounds—but no, that was quite un-English. Dogs lay on mats by winter fires, snoring and stretching, or dogs, trained and alert, stalked the fields with their masters. The friend of man—no, no, not savage.

Maldington was the strange emirate Sir Bill had delegated. Rex had begun to love it. It was his own.

He went on quietly towards his house, reflecting that security had

27

its own conventions, the part of it called cover in particular. 'Project A', for example, was very untypical. It told you nothing and for once it was undramatic, whereas in the war they'd been wildly facetious. There'd been a plan to kidnap Rommel and they'd called it Sunglass; another to recapture the Irish Treaty Ports and that they'd called Bograt.

But they seemed to be growing up. Stumble on the chance of the biggest coup since the original big bang and they called it Project A. Rightly in this case since if the programme succeeded its product would be as conventional as the title. No atoms, no fall out—just an old-fashioned bang in an old-fashioned gunshell but ten or twelve times more powerful than an old-fashioned blockbuster bomb. Superior manpower would be largely neutralized since it wouldn't dare concentrate. And armour—pouff! A rifle grenade would blow a tank a furlong. And all without fall-out, all without that tiresome sense of sin. No men with self-conscious beards, women in dirty jeans, cooling their nates on your doorstep. Just a nice old conventional bang but raised to the power of n. You needn't be a statesman, even a soldier, to realize the implications. And the country which got it first. . . .

Rex's man put the car away and Rex ran a bath. He had been playing golf and was pleasantly tired. He didn't play well but he enjoyed the exercise, and though Project A's programme was something called Crash, it was an absolute rule that every man working on it must have thirty-eight hours leisure a week. Continuous. There was somebody called a welfare officer who shooed them away from Maldington. Wives weren't allowed yet.

Rex looked at his private mail. It had arrived on Saturday evening but he hadn't had time to open it. There wasn't a great deal—bills and some circulars, a letter from a professional association. Irene had had friends and he hadn't much cared for them. They'd left him when she had and she'd scared away his own. He mixed himself a modest whisky, remembering that last time he'd taken a drink or two he'd made rather a fool of himself.

But he'd learnt his lesson cheaply: that was over and done with.

The last letter of the pile was in a thick cream envelope, crested. Rex took out the invitation card, its edges bevelled and gilded. His Excellency the Ambassador requested the pleasure of the company of Mr. Rex Hadley. Six to eight-thirty. R.S.V.P. to the Private Secretary.

There was a note with the invitation card and Rex read it frowning:

Dear Mr. Hadley,

I have been hoping that we might meet again. I believe you said at Sestriere that you were having the first part of a holiday and were intending to go back there. By coincidence I may now be able to do the same. Meanwhile, I hope you will be able to accept the invitation enclosed. A few friends are coming on to my flat afterwards for a stand-up meal, and I shall be delighted if you can be one of them.

Yours sincerely,
Francis de Fleury

Rex's first feeling was of irritation. Damn it, the man was a limpet. Rex wanted no part of de Fleury, nor of de Fleury's world. He had just escaped from an intolerable domesticity and from the frustration in his profession which had gone with a foolish marriage. An allegedly social life around the embassies wasn't what he wanted to replace it. He wanted something else and knew it; he would have admitted by now that it called itself Mary Francom. It was a pity about de Fleury but at least they weren't married. Mary had told him her story: it wasn't for him to blame her if she discreetly looked after herself. The decision to do so owned respectable antiquity, and at his age one shouldn't be a prig. Prigs threw things away, rejecting a chance of happiness on some theory about women. Theories about women were for very young men. Mary wasn't an Englishwoman and she wasn't an intellectual. Irene had been both. Rex had had just about a bellyfull of intellectual Englishwomen.

He sat down with his weak whisky, staring at the invitation card, his irritation fading into something less acceptable. He knew it was uncertainty, almost a foreboding. Mary had told him de Fleury's profession: he was a military attaché, and Rex had been surprised. de Fleury wasn't a rich playboy, or not all the time, and Mary's manner had impressed him. It had been casual enough, but she had looked at him straightly, her grey eyes serious. It might almost have been a warning. Like, he remembered suddenly, something Julian Cohn had said. Besides, the invitation was a little odd—odd in itself. Rex wasn't quite ignorant of the world of diplomats: they didn't waste time on people who couldn't serve them. A feeler or two, a cool assessment, then, for the unimportant, the smoothest of brush-offs. And production engineers, even good ones, were hardly important people in the world of military attachés.

Or were they? he thought uneasily. He was supposed to be in charge of a factory at Maldington, but it was one with barbed wire and dogs, strange buildings and stranger people. There had been much in the Press on Maldington, surmise and guesses.

Rex went to his desk, starting on an immediate refusal. He checked himself. But it was always these snap decisions which landed you in trouble. They looked so easy, obvious; so often they were unwise. Too often you committed yourself.

He'd talk to Mary Francom and he'd ask her advice. They were dining again tomorrow. She'd know about de Fleury and she'd be able to judge his motives. She had every opportunity.

But not for much longer, not for too long.

Major Robert Mortimer was on the telephone, listening very carefully to Macdonald. Macdonald was saying quietly: 'You've an interest in Julian Cohn?'

'We have.'

'And I've an interest in a street accident, on the face of it an ordinary hit-and-run. I told you we'd found nobody who saw it, but I said that we might. And now we have. It was a boy coming back from school. There was rather a nasty mess and he was frightened, so he ran home to mother but held his tongue. Then there was the usual appeal for witnesses on the radio and the family heard it. The boy included. Mother says something like: "That happened pretty close to us", and the boy begins to talk. Father thinks it over—he's a pretty stolid type—but he comes to us this morning.'

'With the number of the car?'

'I wish it were that easy, sir. We haven't the number, but the boy was a car fan and he noticed the make.' There was a tiny pause, then casually: 'It was a DS Citroën.'

'Indeed?'

'Indeed. But we've a little more than that. The boy didn't get the number but he noticed something else as the Citroën drove away from him. He says it was going like a bat out of hell but he noticed the back of it. There was a foreign identification plate—the letters of the country of registration.' A pause again. 'In this case it was a single letter, one pretty early in the alphabet. To me that means nothing special but it might to you.'

Mortimer whistled softly.

'You're interested, sir? As Security Executive?'

'I'm interested but I'm guessing wildly. We often do, you know. I've nothing to give you or I'd swop at once.'

'A pity that, for we've something more to offer you. We've been doing a little police work.' There was the slightest emphasis, faintly ironic, on 'police'. 'Just the boring routine. We've been checking the car ferries just in case. The middle of the winter isn't a busy time for them and it wasn't too difficult.' Macdonald's voice became sud-denly formal, the voice of a senior policeman in a magistrate's court. 'It has been ascertained that on the day of the incident only one car of the make in question and with the foreign identification letter referred to left this country by any ferry. Its number is of course available in the Customs records. These further show that the car in question was brought into this country the day before the accident.'

'You've been busy.'

'We're policemen. And as policemen I should guess we're at the end of it. Of course we've put the machine in gear on the other side but I'll be surprised if it turns up anything useful. . . . A man brings his car over for twenty-four hours, no doubt with a cast iron reason. We'd still be a mile from a case in this country. We've the number of a DS Citroën which came here the day before an accident, and a witness who saw a DS Citroën involved in an accident. *A* DS Citroën, number unknown; *an* accident. Of course there's the identification letter, but no court is going to listen to us if we put up a case which depended on a make of car and a foreign identification letter. There'd be trouble if we even tried. So unless Mr. Cohn comes round again, unless he saw the number and remembers it— pretty unlikely, I'd say—and assuming it wasn't a false one——'

'Cohn's still unconscious?'

'Yes. Mr. Cohn has had rough treatment. We've not much hope in Mr. Cohn, nor for him. Still, if you're still interested. . . .'

'I am.'

'If you're interested, I've something more. But I wouldn't lean too hard on it. It's quite a small thing and it might mean nothing. My informant may be mistaken. . . . You've used these drive-on car ferries yourself, sir?'

'Often.'

'Then you'll know how they work. You drive your car on and round, give the keys to a sort of sailor, and then you walk up to the saloon. Sometimes, when they're not too busy, they pick up a pound or two by doing a wash for you. They weren't at all pushed on the night in question, and there's a man who remembers offering to wash a DS Citroën. There was only one man with it and he declined the wash. Strong foreign accent, which isn't unusual, but there was something which was. Or you may think so. It wouldn't impress a court, though.'

32

'Go on.'

'This car-washer cased the job while the driver was coming in. It struck him as a little odd—so odd he remembered it. The weather was filthy and so was the car. All except that sloping bonnet and the bumper in front. They'd just been washed, and carefully.'

'Thanks,' Mortimer said. 'Thanks very much.'

'Good hunting, sir.'

CHAPTER IV

Rex had taken Mary Francom to dinner in Soho. He was fond of rice and they were eating it—not curry for there was also wine. She noticed that he drank very little and she sensed that he wasn't at ease. They had eaten together twice before and twice he had been relaxed. Both had been happy evenings, enjoyable and something more. But this evening he was tense, forcing himself to action which he had already decided but still found difficult. At length he said: 'You remember Francis de Fleury?'

That put it, she thought, with delicacy.

'I still remember him.'

That put it, she thought, with the candour she felt she owed him. She hated deception for she had seen too much of it.

'And you'll have heard of a place called Maldington. I've already told you I work there because there isn't any point in hiding it. Anybody who wanted to could easily find that out. And you'll have heard rumours about Maldington.'

'Rumours,' she said, 'a good deal of gossip.'

'Yes. But you told me what de Fleury's job was. I was alone at Sestriere and I'd just been appointed to Maldington. That wasn't yet common knowledge but there was nothing secret about the appointment itself, and I suppose it's quite possible that a man in de Fleury's position could hear about it sooner than most. So I was alone at Sestriere on a holiday, and de Fleury knocks my drink over.' Rex

34

hesitated, then went on: 'It's occurred to me that he paid me a lot of attention for a man whose drink he'd spilt.'

'Sestriere is a resort. Perhaps he liked you.' She smiled. 'You're rather a modest man.'

'I'm afraid I was a foolish one.' He looked at her directly but her eyes told him nothing. It was a difficult face to read, serene but determined. The determination he accepted for she'd told him her story. The serenity still surprised him, but he admired it too.

'Go on,' she said.

'I drank too much. Not a skinful—nothing, I dare say, for a man accustomed to champagne—but a little too much for me. It's my impression I talked stupidly.'

The elegant black eyebrows straightened in reflection. He knew she was thinking it over, considering a decision of her own. She was considering her loyalties, though Rex didn't know it. She worked for the Security Executive and personal feeling was something outside her contract. It was in fact fatal to any agent, but she would have admitted that with Rex Hadley emotions weren't wholly absent. She'd leave it at that whilst she could. Choosing her words she said deliberately: 'I think you're right in guessing de Fleury knew about Maldington. I mean that you'd been posted there.'

'And I talked foolishly about the place? I was—well, insecure?' She didn't answer him.

'You must tell me,' he said. He had noticed her hesitation, misunderstanding it. She was a courteous woman; she wouldn't wish to wound a host. He said again sharply: 'Tell me.'

'You mentioned a Project A.'

She saw his face fall, harden again grimly. She knew he was shaken, but his voice was normal. That she respected.

'I didn't realize it was as bad as that.'

'Why so bad?'

'I talked about Maldington—and Project A?'

'Not quite. It was de Fleury who mentioned Maldington You

35

talked about yourself a bit, a brand new job you were obviously looking forward to.'

'But I mentioned Project A?'

'Is that so serious?'

'Not in itself, perhaps. Project A or Plan Twenty-Seven—in itself it gives nothing away beyond a codename. But I'd just been appointed to Maldington and nobody believes that it's really an engineering shop. And the first thing I do is to confirm to three strangers, one of them the military attaché of a not too co-operative Power, that whatever is going on there is secret enough to rate a codeword. That puts it at the lowest.'

'But why put it higher? I can see that you are.'

He didn't deny it. 'What I actually said—that's over and beyond recall. But it wouldn't be good for me if anybody repeated it. If they went to my chairman or even higher I'd be lucky to last the day. It wasn't exactly sensible, not something to make a top man trust me. I get put into my first big job, and promptly I drop one. Nothing fatal but undeniably silly.' Rex shook his head. 'I know what I'd do myself: I'd play it safe and get rid of Hadley quickly. I'd feel I was obliged to. There were yourself and Cohn and de Fleury——'

'You seem to be trusting me.'

'I am.'

'And Julian Cohn is dead.'

'I didn't know that. I've been terribly busy. I haven't read a newspaper for days.'

'It was a street accident. They brought him to my nursing home and there he died.'

It had been an hour ago and she had reported to Robert Mortimer. Cohn hadn't spoken for he hadn't recovered consciousness. Mortimer had been disappointed but not, she felt, excessively. Major Mortimer knew something.

'Which leaves Francis de Fleury, a military attaché. . . .'

Mary said quietly: 'You've something to tell me.'

She liked it that he didn't waste time in comment. He took from his pocket a letter and an invitation card, handing her both. She read them carefully; said with an equal care: 'I could guess what you're wondering.'

'You don't think I'm jumping to conclusions? You don't think I'm scared of nothing?'

She shook her head slowly.

'Then you know de Fleury, you know him well.' It was a statement, quite without private overtones, and for an instant she resented it. She was de Fleury's mistress and Rex was accepting it, coming to de Fleury's mistress for an opinion about the man. She said equally impersonally: 'Oh yes, I know him well.'

'Then you'll know about diplomats too. Do you think he'd ask me to a party simply because he liked me? On the face of it I'm a casual pick-up in the snow, a sort of shipboard acquaintance. And you know how long they last.'

'I think you should go just the same.'

'You do?'

She accepted coffee and drank it thoughtfully. 'In your place I'd want to bring it to a head; I'd want to *test* him. Suppose you go and nothing happens, nothing of what we're thinking. So home you go a happy man. And if Francis should start something, if he should move. . . .'

Her voice died away and he had to prompt her. 'Yes?'

'You'll know what you're in for and that's always an advantage. You'll know where you are.'

'I'll be finished,' he said simply.

'No, Rex, you won't be finished.'

She had looked away, smiling a smile he hadn't seen before. When it was spent she turned to him. The oblique timeless smile, the smile of another race, had puzzled him, but now she was serene again. Rex Hadley drew strength from her. She said again: 'No, Rex, you wouldn't be finished. You're a very nice man. You're

37

considerate and kind and English.' Her voice changed unexpectedly. 'And God, how I'd hate to be your enemy.'

'You'll never be that.' He shook her hand but she slipped it away. It wasn't the moment and perhaps it never would be.

Mary Francom was a scrupulous woman.

He put her into a taxi and this time she took his hand. 'Tell me what happens, Rex. Keep me in touch. I've friends and some useful contacts. I've a certain profession.'

'If you mean about de Fleury I could soon put an end to that.'

She shut the door and he heard her laugh. The sound of it astonished him. Out of the window she waved at him gaily. 'But you don't know what I'm talking about. You haven't an idea.'

Rex walked to the garage where he had parked his modest car, driving back to Maldington reflectively. It was his hunch that an evening at de Fleury's wouldn't be a pleasant one: de Fleury would —what had Mary called it?—move. Rex hadn't a plan but he did have a certain solace. At least he'd made his mind up, or Mary had made it for him. For that he was grateful.

Mary Francom sat in her taxi twisting a glove. It wasn't a gesture she often indulged and she was quite unconscious of it now. She was thinking about Englishmen, trying not to think of Rex as English. . . . An extraordinary breed. You told them your private story, the loss of property and, worse, the right to work; hunger and maybe prison; finally the night journey through the wire and minefields, horrible ex-German things which jumped three feet to blow your crutch out. You told them the story and their faces darkened in anger. It was an injustice—wrong. But somehow they didn't feel it. Why indeed should they? They hadn't been invaded for a thousand years. Of course they'd been mercilessly bombed, but next morning, when they'd swept the glass up, there they still were. There the survivors were—no tanks in the streets, no alien gestapo. You told them what the other thing was like, you made them angry, but it was an impersonal anger, the good man's horror of an evident evil. They didn't experience for they didn't know.

Mary lit a cigarette with quick movements which Rex would not have recognized. It was easy to think of England as a sort of open zoo, an offshore island for fortunate non-Continental animals. It was easy but it was misleading. Rex Hadley, for instance. She'd meant it when she'd said she'd hate to be his enemy.

The oddest men. To women of another race they sometimes seemed less than human. But when you began to look at one, when he *engaged* you. . . .

A woman of another race frowned suddenly. 'Keep me in touch,' she'd said, 'I've friends and some useful contacts.' But she was deeper in than that. She worked for the Security Executive and that meant watching de Fleury. Which meant living with him, taking him, doing what the Executive secretly paid her to do.

It also meant deceiving Rex, or at least the obligation to say nothing. Agents mustn't disclose themselves—that was elementary but absolute. She sighed unhappily. She'd have to pick the hand up, Rex and all. She could guess what de Fleury would do for she'd seen the instrument. It was her business to recognize such things. She had known what it was and now it frightened her. It had been beautifully made and very small. It would go into an inside pocket easily.

She didn't doubt it had.

Rex Hadley arrived at His Excellency's cocktail party rather later than he had intended, for he had been delayed at Maldington. His three top scientists had nobbled him. He had listened carefully though he didn't expect to understand them. He didn't understand the language of pure science but he could adequately translate it. His business was to translate it in terms of machines and power, and, if the thing came off, finally into production. So he had listened patiently, but with a slowly sinking spirit. For this wasn't a move forward or anything like it, it was simply a scientists' quarrel. It was Rex's experience that the jealousies of top scientists were petty and even childish. He accepted the fact as an occupational risk of their profession, but acceptance didn't make it easier to live with. So he listened with patience and he finally decided; he sent them away, not happy, but at least to work again. He would have confessed to disappointment.

Now he walked into the embassy, leaving his coat in the cloak-room. He had been to embassy parties before and had acquired a certain nose for them. They were given in huge old houses in South West One, something between an institute and a very grand under-taker's. As at an undertaker's life was quite absent. Nobody lived in these Victorian palaces though one or two might work there. The food came from caterers, the wine from the country concerned. Even when it was importable. Some wine-snob might take to it ('I picked this up from the Ruritanian embassy—how do you like it?') and no chance of advertisement could nowadays be ignored.

But Rex knew at once that this wasn't that sort of party. This would be well above average, for the embassy belonged to a Power which, if formidably decayed, still knew that it was civilized. Flowers had been used, but sparingly, and all of them were good. There weren't many servants but those there were were native to the house. There was even a smell of cooking, faint but reassuring. When an embassy cooked its own cocktail-eats the party would be exceptional.

Francis de Fleury met him at the head of the splendid staircase. 'I'm delighted you could come,' he said. 'The ambassador's been called away, so I'm sorry you won't meet him.' He led the way to a magnificent sideboard, casual but superbly stocked, taking a bottle by the neck. 'Champagne? I remember you like it.'

Rex said deliberately: 'I have to watch champagne.'

'Really? But this one won't damage you.' de Fleury passed the wineglass, beckoning to a youngish couple. They crossed the room quickly and de Fleury introduced them. 'Well, I must go to work again. Of course we'll be meeting later.'

He drifted away.

Rex chatted easily but he wasn't quite at ease. . . . 'Champagne? I remember you like it,' and 'This one won't damage you.' It might have meant nothing or it might have been considered. Rex sipped the wine slowly.

It was already late and the room was emptying. Presently de Fleury came back again. 'I think we could excuse ourselves, I think we could go on. You know where I live.'

'I'm afraid I don't.'

It was true. de Fleury's letter had been written on official paper.

de Fleury told him politely. 'Would you like me to write it down?'

'No thanks.'

. . . The damned man's pretty sure of himself. He's trying to get me down, one up himself; he's trying to soften me.

We'll see.

Rex went to his car and drove to Chelsea. de Fleury's flat was just off Cheyne Walk, and Rex at last found parking space in Flood Street. He locked the car and walked back quickly. He was excited but not afraid.

The flat was in an Edwardian block, old-fashioned but not uncomfortable. de Fleury let Rex in himself, direct into a corridor. On the right were the principal rooms—dining-room first, then living-room, then the main bedroom. To the left were the other bedrooms and, in the arm of an L at the end of the corridor, bathroom and kitchen. Francis de Fleury led the way into the dining-room.

The cold table was of a simple excellence but Rex was surprised at the company. To begin with it was a much smaller gathering than he had imagined, for there were only three couples present. One he had met at the embassy, the man a colleague of de Fleury's though his junior. The other two hadn't been there—Rex was sure of it. The two women were quietly dressed, but they had an air of cold competence which, twenty years before, Rex felt he could have placed precisely. Today he wasn't so sure. Nor were their men what he would have expected in a military attaché's flat. Their linen was clean and they were polite with a faintly ironical detachment, but clearly they weren't social in any sense at all. They had muscular figures and they moved with an athlete's balance. Rex was reminded of films which he had seen pre-war, films about Chicago and a gangster's bodyguard. But these men were quiet, contemporary. It was certain they weren't gorillas but they might have been a retinue. They weren't there for nothing.

They ate their supper talking of nothing in particular. There was more champagne but Rex declined. He noticed that de Fleury didn't press him. Nobody was paying him special attention but he was conscious that he was central. The others had been told about him, *knew*.

Knew what? He'd soon find out.

Presently de Fleury looked at his watch. 'It's half past ten and there's an hour to kill. I'll run you some films.' He turned to Rex Hadley. 'This,' he said deliberately, 'this you'll find interesting.'

They went into the living-room. There were already a screen and projector readied. They sat down in two rows and de Fleury turned the lights out. He showed them snow scenes—Sestriere and much else. It was very good photography. They watched for perhaps a quarter of an hour, then de Fleury broke the silence.

'Rather good, don't you think?'

The man beside Rex said promptly: 'It's a pity there's no sound.'

The three women rose instantly and the man from the embassy. The words had been a cue.

'We must be going now.'

Rex rose in turn. 'I think I must be going too. I've a long drive home.'

The man at his side had risen too. 'Not yet,' he said. His hand on Rex's shoulder was polite but firm.

Rex Hadley sat down again.

de Fleury showed the others out, came back into the living-room. 'Somebody was saying it was a pity we had no sound?'

'Yes, I said that.'

'But we have. I made a tape at Sestriere, a very good one too.'
Rex heard a tape recorder start, a preliminary blurr of voices.

The front door bell rang suddenly.

de Fleury switched the recorder off, walking away swearing.
When he returned it was with Mary Francom. She seemed to be
tight and de Fleury was saying icily: 'But it's Thursday, I assure
you.'

'Thursday or Friday, all the same to Mary.'

'Not the same to me.'

Mary looked round the room. 'Of course if you've got grand
friends. . . .'

'I wouldn't call them that. Mr. Hadley, perhaps. You know Mr.
Hadley—you met at Sestriere.'

'Hiya,' she said.

Rex bowed uncertainly. He couldn't make it out.

'Now give a girl a drink.'

'I really think——'

'Give a girl a nightcap.'

de Fleury shrugged, going back to the dining-room, returning
with a wineglass. 'Drink that and beat it.'

'Pretty manners tonight.'

'I told you it was Thursday.'

'Oh, all right. I can take a polished hint.' Mary finished the wine.
'Good night,' she said. She turned unsteadily and de Fleury went
with her. At the front door there was an exchange of unpleasantries
in a language Rex didn't know.

He heard the door shut crisply.

On the landing Mary waited. When she could hear that a tape
recorder had started again she took her shoes off and, from her
bag, her key. She let herself into the flat again, moving noiselessly
down the corridor, carrying her shoes. The living-room was open
still but nobody was facing it. She slipped past it silently, going on

43

to the bedroom next door. She was perfectly sober but she put herself to bed. She knew where her things were.

She left the door open, settling to listen intently.

The blurr of voices from the tape machine began again, cleared suddenly to recognizable speech. There was de Fleury's but there was also Rex's.

It was a good deal worse than he had feared. He knew that tape recordings could be forged, but this one hadn't been fabricated, only edited with wicked skill. He heard himself say Project A, a bitter confirmation, and Maldington was mentioned too, not by himself but by de Fleury. Not that it mattered. The interpolation had been cunningly done, the clear impression was that de Fleury had asked questions about Maldington and that Rex had answered them. There were cunning repetitions, sentences out of context, a good deal of laughter much louder than Rex's normal laugh. The tape ran three minutes but it was wholly damning. It was the tape of a drunken braggart talking inexcusably.

de Fleury ran it twice, his eyes never leaving Rex's. Then he said coldly: 'I think you'll understand.'

Rex didn't answer. There was nothing to say.

'But we'd better have it clear—unmistakably clear. I want everything you do at Maldington—but everything. How you're progressing and what you've found. And how you plan to exploit your breaks.'

Rex Hadley had risen. 'You do?'

de Fleury pointed at the tape machine. 'You know what that could do to you. In your sort of job things don't depend on proof, on persuading some court that evidence is genuine. The slightest suspicion would be enough. The slightest suspicion and——'

'I dare say you're right.'

'I know I'm right.' de Fleury walked to the door, holding it in dismissal. 'Every week at first, please, and more frequently later.

That depends on how it goes. *I'll* decide that. You'll always find me here on Thursday evenings.' He looked at the other two men, and his confident voice changed smoothly to menace. 'You'll always find us here.'

'All of you?'

'All that I need. I've friends, you see, and you'd do well to remember it. Just in case it crossed your mind that I was bluffing. So I've friends and you haven't. If it came to any unpleasantness you can't get help. You don't dare tell a soul a thing. You're quite alone. Good night.'

Rex walked to his car in Flood Street, driving back to Maldington. de Fleury had been impressively sure of himself; he'd gone to the limit at once. The limit of demand but not of action. This was only the start.

Half an hour later de Fleury went to bed. He had allowed himself a final drink, considering he had earned it. He walked into his bedroom and stopped in his tracks. Then he went to the bed and shook Mary Francom roughly.

'What are you doing here?'

She looked at him through sleep-dimmed eyes. She'd been rubbing them for some time.

'I was asleep.'

He swore at her, went back into the living-room. She heard the tape recorder start, then de Fleury returned to the bedside. The voices were very clear. For an instant he listened, then strode away quickly. The recorder stopped and he was back again.

'You left the door open?'

'I don't sleep in public. You've just opened it yourself.'

He muttered and stalked away again, starting the machine once more, and when he returned he shut the door behind him. Now voices were audible but not the words.

'Francis, what are you playing at?'

He looked at her in fury. 'You're sure you were asleep?'

'Of course I was. I was tight as a tick and I couldn't find a taxi. I had to sleep it off.'

'I've never seen you tight before.'

'You've never seen me desperate. Sometimes it all comes back at me and then I drink.'

He looked at her again. She was warm with sleep, warm and a woman and she still seemed a little drunk.

Under the sheet she moved deliberately. It was suddenly tight around her. 'Francis. . . .'

He began to undress.

She'd never been more charming, for Miss Francom owned a private pride. When she must do a thing at least she would do it well.

CHAPTER V

In his agreeably untidy room in the Security Executive Colonel Charles Russell was recapitulating to Mortimer. 'So Cohn is dead and he didn't talk.'

'I doubt if it much matters, sir. Though of course I can't prove it I'm morally sure they killed him.' Robert Mortimer was remembering Macdonald's 'Good hunting'. It had been an irony verging on sarcasm. There would be, there could be, no hunting, good or bad. If the police couldn't solve an ordinary hit-and-run then Mortimer would be equally helpless in a very unordinary hit-and-run committed by what he believed was a very unordinary foreigner now safely returned to his own country. For all the guesses pointed at planned and deliberate action. So ring up a colleague across the Channel, invoke the Old Friends' Act, and your colleague would be charming. He'd promise co-operation and that would be the end of it.

One didn't betray one's own employees.

Russell said reflectively: 'All right, they killed him. Who did and why? I know, of course. I just want to hear your mind work.'

'I don't think it was de Fleury—killing isn't his style at all. I doubt if he was even told. It was Victor who had motive since what was basically at risk was the fact that Victor was interested in Project A. de Fleury was only an agent, but if somebody blew the agent he would blow the intention too. And Cohn looked like blowing it.

Cohn was a man of the far, far left, and Victor would know it too. So here's a way-out journalist tagging de Fleury at Sestriere, listening to him twisting Hadley, refusing to be shaken off. I dare say Victor simply thought that Cohn was a rival agent, one working for east Europe, or he may have found out that he had made an appointment with me. We'll never know now what Cohn was going to tell me but it may have been the truth. That wouldn't be inconsistent with extreme left wing views because if there's one country which a man of the left wouldn't trust with Project A it's Victor's. They think of it as fascist. But on either assumption Cohn could have been danger-ous to Victor. Not would be—could. Victor thinks in probabilities, percentages of risk. I don't suppose he cares about de Fleury. de Fleury is an agent and expendable: what would matter to Victor would be somebody else discovering that he was actively after Project A. And something of the *how*. I mean that de Fleury had begun to work on Hadley.'

Russell nodded approvingly. 'Very clear thinking. So the hypo-thesis at bottom is that Victor means business. Killing a man who you think can fix one of your agents is worth it only in two cases: that you value the agent exceptionally highly or—more likely, this —that breaking the agent will somehow break you too. You and your intention. Otherwise it's easier simply to switch agents. To commit yourself to killing and in another country—that's putting the biggest chips down. Victor wouldn't do that for nothing but he would for Project A.'

'Then what about de Fleury, sir?'

'We can't act for the moment and I don't think we need to. de Fleury has a plan, a typical blackmailer's plan. Miss Francom, you tell me, has just confirmed it. That was very smooth work indeed. So de Fleury's on the squeeze-game and Rex Hadley's in the pincers.' Russell rubbed his chin. 'Pressure,' he said, 'increasing pressure.'

'But what sort of increase?'

'How do you see it yourself?'

'I'm afraid pretty dimly. de Fleury has a tape of an indiscretion of

Hadley's which could be highly compromising. That puts it at the minimum. But his demand was for immediate information about Project A and for continuing information as the thing progresses. Hadley, in fact, would be simply de Fleury's spy. There's a weapon of course, but it doesn't seem big enough.'

'de Fleury may think that too.'

'Sir?'

'He's timing it—he can afford to. Nothing remarkable has happened yet at Maldington, so why should he rush things? It's a question of technique, and he hasn't always been a military attaché, far less a colonel. So first comes the shock, the outrageous demand. de Fleury has made it. According to Miss Francom he told Hadley to report to him on Thursday, but I doubt if he really expects him to. But when he doesn't de Fleury won't leave it there. He's an experienced hand and a shrewd judge of men; he has enough on Rex Hadley to lose him his job, but that would scarcely guarantee an instant treason. No, he'll build up the squeeze on Hadley, we don't yet know how, but de Fleury will aim to *weaken* him, to scare him too if he thinks that line's worth trying, and he'll hope that when the break comes at Maldington he'll have Hadley broken too. It's a competent, professional ploy. It does need time, though.' Charles Russell knocked his pipe out. 'de Fleury,' he said, 'is much cleverer than his master. I suspect Victor knows it.'

'I hope he does.'

'Meaning?'

'He had Cohn killed—I'm sure of it. de Fleury would never have risked it.'

Charles Russell frowned. Cohn's murder had annoyed him. Of course Cohn had had it coming: sometime and somewhere the Julian Cohns were killed. They never seemed to know it, though. It would never have occurred to Julian Cohn that if and when the system he supported came to power he would be messily liquidated rather before the chairman of the Conservative Party. The left wing intellectuals bought it first: all revolutions proved that. Still, he'd been a citizen and he'd been murdered in Russell's bailiwick. Victor had been impertinent before, but this was something more. Charles Russell wasn't pleased and his cool voice showed it.

'So Victor stepped in across de Fleury; he had Cohn killed. All right. But why should he kill Hadley?'

'I wasn't suggesting killing, sir, or not as an end in itself.'

'Then what were you suggesting?'

'Well. . . . Suppose there were an unexpected breakthrough at Maldington, and in that sort of fusing of science and engineering it's always a possibility. And suppose it came before de Fleury was ready, before he felt certain he had Hadley softened for the final kill. That would be a new situation, wouldn't it? What you called the timing would have changed. de Fleury's timing. Victor might be tempted again.'

'He might. Go on.'

'I was thinking about Dortmund.'

Charles Russell sat immobile. The affair at Dortmund had shocked him and he wasn't easily shocked. It hadn't happened in his territory, he wasn't personally involved, but it had given him for Victor an emotion he wasn't used to. He felt for professional rivals either respect or contempt, assessing them impersonally according to their competence. Provided, that is, they weren't quite savages. But Dortmund had been detestable, a barbarism. Four of Victor's men had crossed the frontier and beaten to pulp an elderly research worker. He'd been found in his car at night with injuries wholly disgusting. He'd died next day and it wasn't quite certain whether he had talked or not: all that was certain was that six months later the army which had begotten Victor was flaunting an automatic mortar which the research worker had been developing. Suspicion of Victor had been equally automatic; there'd been an international outcry but nothing had been proved.

Nothing had been proved and nothing would be. Nothing had been proved of Julian Cohn.

Russell said: 'Dortmund—yes, I follow you.' His voice was one which Mortimer seldom heard. 'If Maldington made a break-through we'd be back on familiar ground. There'd be a secret, in fact—an orthodox, transmissible secret. A handful of men would know it and all would be targets. The boss would be the best of all.'

'You put it pretty crisply, sir.'

'I meant to put it crisply. What's the present position at Maldington?'

'Nothing definite yet. But there's an Indian, a mathematician, and they've sent him to talk to Moltesen in Denmark. And one of the top physicists has been flown to Zurich. You know who lives at Zurich.'

'There's a certain activity?'

'Yes. And not the sort you can hide. You can't send eminent scientists travelling round Europe in disguise. If you try you just make it more noticeable.'

Russell said slowly: 'I don't much like it. It's the sort of situation made for a man like Victor. He might find it irresistible. Like Cohn. Poor Cohn was a precedent, a warning too. We know our Victor.'

'Should I warn Rivers-Legge?' Lieutenant-Commander Rivers-Legge was something called Security Officer at Maldington. The capitals defined him perfectly. He wasn't important to real security.

'Good heavens, no. He's adequate for his job, which is passes and those frightful dogs, and which paper you read on Sunday. But for this sort of thing he'd be quite outgunned. Who else have we there —the proper ones?'

'Twenty at least. It's quite a list.'

'Anyone good for rough stuff?'

'They weren't picked for that.'

'There's that manservant of Hadley's—Perkins. I planted him there myself. He's been trained. What have you told him?'

'Nothing about the blackmail, sir. I didn't think he needed it. So nothing about that tape.'

'Continue to tell him nothing about the tape. But see that he's alerted for his job.'

Major Mortimer made a note.

'And Hadley, now—does he go out much? Does he go driving alone?'

'He goes golfing on Sundays, and sometimes he drives to London.'

'Alone?'

'He doesn't bring her back with him. Not yet.'

'He comes back alone in the dark then?'

Robert Mortimer nodded.

'See that the practice ceases.'

Mortimer went back to his room. He telephoned to Maldington, and he made another call. The voice at the other end said finally: 'I get it—a standing patrol. Starting tomorrow night.'

'I'll join you myself the first time out.'

'Okay.'

Robert Mortimer rang back to Russell. He had expected approval and he received it. Then he grinned. A senior desk man, he adored cloak and dagger.

In a room on the other side of the Channel the man they called Victor was talking to a subordinate.

'Anything from de Fleury?'

'Yes, sir.' The subordinate held a report out.

Victor read it carefully. 'I don't think too much of that.'

'It follows the plan as agreed. It's an excellent start. But excellent.'

'Start! We're in a hurry, man.'

Victor's opinion of de Fleury was that he was a well-bred softie. He was an adequate working spy in circles where most of Victor's agents—Victor himself—would hardly have been at ease, and he therefore had his uses; but when it came to the crunch de Fleury wasn't to be relied on. It was an instinct rooted in the mistrust of the self-made man for anyone who wasn't, and it was quite unjustified. de Fleury in his different way was ruthless.

de Fleury's opinion of Victor, long gestating, was that he was without finesse, a hothead and, in the pinches, simply a barbarian.

Victor asked now: 'What's happening at Maldington?'

'Nothing in particular. There's a scientist visiting Denmark and another gone to Switzerland.'

'You call that nothing?'

'I call it nothing definite.'

'*I* do. Hadley wouldn't send top-flight scientists padding round Europe for nothing. I don't say he's got a breakthrough yet; I say he's got *something*, enough for our people to work on.' Parodying the tall man at their earlier meeting Victor said precisely: 'We've got to have this English thing, we've got to have it too.' He returned to his normal manner. 'Never mind the Marshal, though. The point at the moment is that Hadley will know something. Hadley will have knowledge and I want it. We've got Jacques and Pierre and the man they call Smithy. They're not paid for nothing. They're not retained to decorate de Fleury's little parties, which is how he seems to use them, nor even to hint at the possibility of violence. They're paid to do the rough work and the sooner the better. I say again: Hadley must have knowledge. Get it.'

'There's a considerable risk. Those three are valuable men, and it would be a once-for-all commitment.'

'They mustn't be caught and Hadley mustn't be killed. Better if he isn't. Just made to talk—but quickly. Some journey in a car at night.' Victor rose irritably, striding his room. 'The merest routine,' he said.

'Suppose they're not caught but recognized?'

'They know the quick-escape route. It's always kept open.'

'I suggest we hold Smithy back. He's English and specially useful. Two should be plenty.'

'Very well.' Victor shrugged. He was a dedicated man with the over-simplified ideas of dedication and its instant decisions. He began to write quickly, passing what he had written to his subordinate.

The subordinate read it. 'Don't you really think, sir . . . so early in the developments? Couldn't it be a little crude, a little too risky too soon. In England——"

'Do as you're told and send it.'

The other read the message again, noting the address and frowning.

It wasn't Francis de Fleury's.

Robert Mortimer was enjoying himself. He escaped from his papers seldom, but when he could make the least excuse he did so. His excuse tonight was that they hadn't thought Perkins adequate—not by himself, not quite alone against the resources of a man like Victor. So the Executive had made its own arrangements. He was conscious that they were good ones, conscious too that that was anything but a reason for his own intrusion. The crew of the old Lagonda were extremely expert.

They had picked up the black saloon a mile or two after the junction of the minor road to Maldington with the main to London. They had nothing against it but instinct. There were a driver and another man and certainly they weren't hurrying. At one in the morning on an empty road most people did.

The open Lagonda had an old-fashioned tonneau cover, and what was underneath it was surprising. There was an elaborate short-wave radio and a man at its dials, delicately searching. Robert picked up a microphone.

'Anything doing?'

'Not yet.'

Robert changed gear. He didn't intend to get too close behind the black saloon.

They had driven another mile perhaps when a light on the dashboard went red. Robert picked up the microphone again, and a calm but urgent voice said:

'Got it. There's an operator with a two-way somewhere near the junction. I'm picking up his message.'

'What was the message?'

'A Rapier had just gone past him. It turned off for Maldington along this road. He gave the number—Hadley's. There were two men aboard.'

'Was there an answer?'

'Only a thank you. Not in English.'

'You can't say where it came from?'

'Of course I can't. It's cramped enough in here without D.F. But it came to me loud and clear.'

Robert looked at the black saloon. It was slowing rather quickly, waving him to pass, then, as he didn't, accelerating fiercely.

Robert said to the man beside him: 'Searchlight.'

The black saloon was in a formidable beam.

Across the rear window somebody pulled a curtain. The saloon didn't slow.

Robert looked at his speedometer. 'There's something in hand but not on this road.'

'That goes for them too. At least we're not losing them.'

The curtain of the black saloon was suddenly torn aside. Above the whine of the slipstream there was a crash as the glass was broken. It fell on the road but Mortimer didn't swerve. There was a hand at the gaping window, half a face, and the outline of a gun. In the searchlight's glare the flash was near-invisible.

Robert Mortimer nodded and his passenger bent down. He come up with an automatic rifle, pointing it through the open windscreen.

Robert said: 'Yes,' and the other fired.

Jacques wasn't frightened, only impressed. He had noticed the Lagonda for some time. . . . Two men in cloth caps and scarves, the windscreen open. . . . Lunatics. The English sporting motorist, an almost vintage car. They couldn't be police and far less agents. They simply didn't smell of it.

And now it was clear they were. They knew their business too, the man with the rifle notably. He was shooting in sparing bursts, controlled, professional. There was a tiny wipe of flame, then pause, then a deliberate burst again. Jacques wasn't scared for this was England. They wouldn't be shooting at him but he knew what they were shooting for. And they were bound to get one. Some form of armour-piercing possibly. Not that it mattered.

He felt the nearside tyre go suddenly, shouted at Pierre. Pierre braked, fought his wheel. The black saloon rolled ominously, hesitating almost humanly. Finally it slid into the ditch.

The Lagonda drew alongside and three men sprang out. One had the automatic rifle, the second a pistol. Both carried their weapons with the air of men who knew them. It was something Jacques recognized at once. Further shooting would be suicide. The third man was unarmed. He said politely: 'First put your guns down.'

Two pistols dropped together.

'Jacques and Pierre?'

They didn't answer.

'I'm quite sure you must be. My name's Robert Mortimer.' Robert went to the back of the black saloon, walking behind the firearms. Their owners stood perfectly still, intent and watchful.

Robert returned. 'It's not badly ditched at all. You can probably get her out alone and we'll help you if we have to. There's a tyre you won't get much for, but we haven't touched the spare.'

Jacques looked at Pierre. 'I don't understand.'

'You don't have to understand. I don't want a fuss, that's all. I've standing instructions to avoid political complications.' Mortimer's voice changed sharply. 'Just get the car out and the spare fixed—fast. There's a friend of ours in a Rapier fifteen miles behind us. You know that too, but I want to keep this private.'

Pierre asked: 'And then?'

'Then beat it for Lymington. That's where you go from, isn't it? It's a nice little river and you've a nice little craft. We know all about your arrangements. We've even checked up for you, and they seem to be ready.'

'It's a trick. We'll move and you'll shoot us down. Escaping.'

Robert said patiently: 'I'd shoot you down now if I wanted to and make up excuses later.' He was suddenly exasperated. 'Can't you fools see it? Putting it bluntly your room is much less awkward than your company. If you *force* it on us, well. . . .' Unexpectedly he was Major Mortimer again. 'I hope I don't sound rude.'

Six minutes later they were watching the tail-light of the black saloon. Robert looked at his watch. 'Get the car under cover.'

They drove the Lagonda into a farm track, backing it to face the road, lighting up contentedly. Ninety seconds later a Rapier went by smoothly.

'Awkward if he'd seen it all. Pretty close timing.' It was the man with the rifle.

The man with the gun had another angle. 'George Perkins was with him. Poor George. He'd be mad if he knew. He hates missing parties.'

Robert said grimly: 'I dare say he'll still come in for one.'

CHAPTER VI

Earlier that evening Russell had been dining with Sir William Banner, though he had made the appointment with a certain reluctance. He could be very tough indeed when it was necessary, but he had a strong sense of justice and he was a considerate man; he hadn't seen it as his duty to volunteer to an industrialist that one of his executives had been talking in a fashion which might lead to trouble. *Might* lead to trouble. Charles Russell had taken a familiar decision. He was paid to run security or at least the most delicate part of it, but he wasn't paid to be a busybody, to prejudice other men, probably lose them their jobs, merely to play safe himself. He took pride that he wasn't a civil servant. But now it was certain that trouble had really broken Russell hadn't hesitated; he had contacted Sir William promptly.

They weren't close friends but they had met before, and they had been eating together comfortably. They were civilized men and they hadn't talked business at table, but now they were in Russell's casual room in the Security Executive. Russell was crisp and grey, the model of the soldier turned civilian, Sir William was bald and affable, looking more like a prosperous pawnbroker than the top-flight tycoon he was. When they were settled over a formidable decanter, Russell passed Banner a half sheet of foolscap. He never explained for it wasted time; he wrote down the facts and let his man read them. Then he waited for comment.

Sir William read the half sheet twice. He was looking entirely miserable, the unhappy child he wasn't. Then he said slowly: 'It's bad—I can see it's bad. I give Hadley this Project A, and I don't have to say what that is. Then I send him away on the first leg of a holiday, and he celebrates it by talking too much. About Project A, and to the military attaché of another Power. From our point of view the worst but one. Who then neatly tapes the indiscretion and uses it to blackmail Hadley.' Sir William looked at Russell. 'I suppose I mustn't ask it but maybe it would help. I suppose I mustn't ask you how you know.'

'You can ask it by all means. Moreover I'll tell you since it's a necessary part of the story. We've been watching de Fleury for weeks, his contacts and most things about him. I knew you'd sent Hadley to Maldington though I didn't know you'd pushed him away on holiday.' Russell smiled blandly. 'You were a little too quick for us. In any case we weren't watching Hadley but de Fleury. de Fleury is a military attaché but he's also a common spy. The latter is his profession, the former his cover. And his protection too, since of course he's a diplomat.'

'Then surely you could chuck him out. Have him recalled if that sounds better.'

'Perhaps. And at a pinch. But it isn't so easy. Having a diplomat blacked, made *persona non grata*, isn't so simple. Diplomatists hang together. The usual theory favours a plain conceit—their depreciated profession against the vulgar world outside it. But I don't think it's as slick as that.' Russell crossed his legs, tilting his chair. 'Are you interested?'

'Very.'

'Then I think it's more practical, more reputable in a sense. Consider. It's a very small world, diplomatists', in London or anywhere else. They know what the other man does, and they know who does what in the Foreign Office. So you're sitting in the Foreign Office, a pretty senior man; you're looking at the final plums but so are a lot of others. Moreover there aren't so many, or not the really juicy ones. And a blacking case comes up to you, somebody whom those tiresome fellows in the Security Executive, or maybe M.I.5, would like to see the back of. They've a plateful of evidence or they wouldn't be putting it up, though it's unlikely to be conclusive. Now you don't take the final decision, but your opinion is well thought of. There won't be a recall, even a discreetly arranged transfer, unless you recommend it to the top. So what do you do?'

'Your duty, I hope.'

'Oh quite. But you're also human. It's perfectly well known in your own absurd world that this sort of case comes up across your desk. So you black Mr. X of country Y, or rather you recommend it. Country Y won't be pleased with you. They won't complain, they can't, but they've a dozen ways of showing it. And one of them can be serious, for six months later Her Majesty's ambassador to Y gets knifed in a snooty brothel. But *you* won't be in the running for the job. And suppose you've had an unlucky spell; suppose I've been tiresome or my colleagues have; suppose you've had a *string* of cases, six, say, or seven, and done your strict duty in all of them. That's six jobs or seven in six or seven countries—gone. You're not even a starter for any of them. Remember you've a career to nurse. *They've* got the jobs: *you* want them.'

Banner was staring at Colonel Charles Russell. Russell had the reputation of considerable means; he wasn't ambitious and honours he despised; he could afford to indulge a sardonic humour.

The trouble with that one was that Russell looked wholly serious. On an inflexion of inquiry Sir William said: 'A most interesting theory.'

But Russell wasn't rising. 'I'm glad I haven't bored you.'

'It would explain a great deal. Recent cases, the F.O. scandals——'

'It was meant to explain why de Fleury is here still. We'd have been watching him in any case. On principle.'

'And I gather you have. Discovering that Hadley talked to him, discovering that de Fleury made a highly compromising tape of it.' Sir William sighed softly for he liked and respected Rex

Hadley. 'And now I suppose you'll be asking me to sack him.'

'What a damned fool idea.'

Sir William wasn't offended. His giggle was of pure relief. Russell had heard it before and it had ceased to astonish him. Banner asked quickly: 'Why?'

'Why on earth should you sack him?'

'It's the orthodox reaction.'

'Fiddle, my dear chap. And reaction's a dreadful word. There would be just two reasons to get rid of him: first that you thought he'd leaked on purpose and second that you thought him hopelessly insecure. Psychologically and permanently.'

'I don't think either of them.'

'Good. Because there's a third excellent reason not to sack him. On my side, that is. We know our opponent and we know what he wants. That's information about Project A—confirmation of what it is, and with luck how it's developing. Later there might be more, something technical perhaps, something commonly called a secret. So you'll see what I'm getting at. We know about de Fleury and we know what he wants, but our special advantage is that we also know the immediate means he's chosen. In military language, which isn't always as woolly as you imagine, we know his first objective. Which is a man called Rex Hadley. So sack him and we're in the dark again. Knowing what he does about Hadley, de Fleury is going to think it distinctly suspicious if he suddenly disappears without explanation. That would warn de Fleury—warn him that we knew something. He'd be very unlikely to attack again in a position he knows is strongly held. Forgive me the jargon. So he'd try somewhere else and we'd be guessing at it.' Russell rose, pouring from the decanter. 'Sack Hadley and you do me a disservice.'

Banner considered it, lighting one of the twenty-five. There had been a cigar after dinner but that didn't count. At last he said: 'But that makes Hadley a sort of bait. A stalking horse.'

'You'd sack him then—for safety's sake? You think he'd approve of that?'

'I've a feeling you're too quick for me. I'm glad I don't trade with you.'

'A compliment. I thank you.'

'Then how do you see it developing?'

'Blackmail—you used the word yourself. The classic pattern.'

'What pattern is that?'

'Pressure—increasing pressure.' Russell was conscious that he had employed the phrase before, but he wasn't a man who paid much attention to what grammarians called elegant variation. When words were useful he used them for their usefulness. He said again: 'Increasing pressure.'

'But Hadley could end it at any time he chose. Hadley could tell me everything.'

'And lose his job?'

'We've just decided otherwise.'

'He wouldn't know that.'

Sir William nodded, thinking it over. When he had done so he said deliberately: 'I suppose Hadley could still tell me—throw himself on my mercy if the cliché doesn't offend you. But I don't think he will. As it happens I would have fought for him tooth and nail. I'd have had to report it, to you I mean, but I'd have done my best to save him. But he wouldn't guess that. He's a quiet sort of man, not the type to assume that an employer is going to do him favours which he hasn't the right to ask for. He was born before the welfare state was thought of.'

'So you think he'll say nothing? He'll stick it alone?'

'I think he'll try, at any rate for the present. He's pleasant and easy to like but there's a mighty hard core to him. He's half an Ulsterman. There's a protestant streak which a catholic can respect.'

'That's my impression too.'

'Then where do we go from here? You don't yourself want Hadley sacked and I can follow the reason. For different reasons nor do I. But what are we going to *say* to him? I assume we'll have to tell him that we know.'

'I'd rather not tell him anything.'

Sir William said sharply, suddenly the tycoon: 'That means you suspect him. You're going to have him watched.'

'I am not.'

Charles Russell went silent. He had a horror of secret police and a vast knowledge of them. Whilst he lived the Executive would never be that. Contemporary treason bred contemporary security. Russell regretted the birth but at least he could control the child. So never a secret police—never whilst he lived. A secret police, self-begotten and self-perpetuating, inhuman by definition since its end was not the state it was supposed to serve but in practice its own survival. The Executive snooped—spied if you preferred the word. It was obliged to. It painstakingly built up dossiers on hundreds of innocent people. But that was the essence: they were *innocent* people. Russell insisted on it tirelessly. He had an officeful of paper on people who were innocent till somebody proved them guilty; he snooped only when obliged to and then with reluctance. Charles Russell was sixty and more, old-fashioned and not ashamed of it; he wouldn't have been flattered to be called a fair-minded man but nor would he have been offended to be thought one.

He said firmly: 'I don't suspect Hadley and we're already watching de Fleury. That is enough.'

'I'm delighted to hear it, but it still leaves the question. What do we say to Hadley?'

'Nothing. Nothing at all.'

'I don't think I follow. Aren't you going to tell him that we know?'

Charles Russell shook his head.

'Why not?'

'Call it experience. Half a lifetime in security.'

'That isn't an answer.'

'Perhaps. . . . May I ask you a question?'

'If it helps to answer mine.'

It was becoming a little clearer why Sir William was a tycoon.

63

'Then suppose you were Hadley and suppose the Executive spoke to you. Could you put it behind you? Could you behave quite normally?'

'Probably not.'

'Wouldn't you look over your shoulder? Wouldn't you, well, *inhibit* things? Developments in fact. It's those that interest me.'

Sir William exploded suddenly. 'You're a damned unscrupulous man.'

Charles Russell didn't flinch but he suppressed a sigh. It struck him as very unfair but he was used to unfairness; in a sense he was paid to accept it; he said evenly: 'But you're entitled to know the position. *You* are.'

'On that we can agree at least.' Sir William was rather cool.

'I'm glad of that. So I've an agent covering de Fleury, a woman. She was with him when Hadley talked foolishly and she contrived to be present again when he played the tape back at him. Hadley met her at Sestriere when she was under de Fleury's protection but he seems to have taken a considerable fancy to her. Be that as it may, they've been meeting since they both returned from holiday— holiday, that is, for Hadley. The lady was on a job for us. But Hadley doesn't know that, nor will she tell him since she's a trained and professional agent. So we've an agent covering de Fleury and an agent privately meeting Hadley.' Russell smiled urbanely. 'It's extremely convenient they're the same woman agent.'

Sir William said softly: 'Christ.' He looked at Charles Russell with a very odd expression. It wasn't contempt but it might almost have been pity. He lit a cigarette again though he was running ahead of ration; he picked up Russell's précis, re-reading it methodically. When he had finished he spoke again. 'A man has been killed lest he compromise de Fleury. I gather you can't prove it but I accept it myself. And there were some very queer guests at de Fleury's flat. Your agent noticed them. I dare say you've a word for them though it might not be mine. And all this is covered by a single woman. You talked about developments and it's not a word I liked. If it goes beyond blackmail you're solely responsible. If it moves into violence, danger. . . .'

'You're thinking about protection?'

'It's a word like another. You know what I'm thinking.'

'Rex Hadley has an important job. It was important, interesting to the Executive, quite apart from what happened at Sestriere.'

Sir William looked up quickly, but Russell was pouring the last of the decanter. He held the wine against the light, admiring it, then he smiled at Sir William Banner. 'You remember Rex Hadley's couple? You were thoughtful about that. You interviewed them first, I think.'

'And how did you know that?'

'They came from a London agency. They also came from me. You mustn't press me for detail but I'll tell you that's the least of it.'

Sir William rose swiftly and held out his hand. He walked to the door and at it he turned. 'Good-bye,' he said, 'and thank you for dinner. That I enjoyed.'

Two hours later the telephone woke Russell noisily. He listened to Robert Mortimer, at length said decidedly: 'You did well. We don't want a scandal—politically it's the worst possible moment for it—and in any case there's more of this to come. Much more if I'm guessing rightly, and in our trade nothing's worse than a premature showdown. In writing tomorrow, please, and meanwhile congratulations. Good night.'

Russell had gone peacefully to sleep again.

But Rex Hadley had not. He had reached his house at half-past one, both safely and in ignorance of danger, but he did not sleep. He lay quietly but miserably, thought chasing its tail round an evening in London which had distressed him.

It had begun with a surprise. He had been backing his car out when George Perkins had walked up to him. Perkins was an ex-Marine, though Rex didn't know it, a fresh-faced man who held himself superbly. He was wearing his best suit and a hard white collar, and he asked a little sheepishly: 'Were you going to London, sir? I was wondering if you'd give me a lift.' Perkins looked at his shoes. 'I've a pretty heavy date there.'

'I'll be coming back very late.'

'That suits me too, sir.'

They arranged where to meet and when.

An hour and a half later Rex had been dining again with Mary Francom. By now they had a table by prescription, and the waiter brought martinis without the order. Rex noticed that she had changed her hair. It made her look younger. A comma of smooth dark hair above one eyebrow, apparently careless, cunningly considered, was the cipher of a first-class hairdresser. Rex looked at her approvingly. He had a proposition to make to Mary Francom and he made it quite simply.

She took it as he had thought she would, coolly and without protest. But she didn't accept. Instead she said calmly: 'You know what I really want, Rex?'

'No.' It wasn't quite true.

'I want money and I'm saving it. I dare say that sounds middle class, but I'm a middle-class woman. Then I want British nationality.'

'That shouldn't be difficult. You've been here six years. You're a nurse and we're short of them.'

She shook her head. 'I'm a Hungarian.'

'But we're rather pro Hungarians.'

She looked at him sadly. 'You were. But you soon got disillusioned. After the trouble there was a flood of us, and you couldn't have been nicer. We were freedom-fighters, heroes—bah! What you got was a load of layabouts, people who saw an unexpected chance and took it. One in thirty had heard a shot fired.' Her mouth moved sideways in a smile he hadn't seen. 'You soon saw through us.'

'But you weren't a layabout.'

'Perhaps.'

He waited, lighting her cigarette. She had something else to say and it was his instinct that she would say it. This evening she needed to talk. Presently she went on.

'We're pretty shabby people, pretty feckless. We've always been pushed around, and mostly we've deserved it.' She managed a normal smile. 'I've German blood myself, so perhaps I'm not quite hopeless.'

'I don't think you're hopeless at all.'

'No, but I'm tainted, tarred.'

'With what?'

She didn't answer directly. 'There was a man, another Hungarian. He was a writer, an exile. He says he's a writer, though nobody seems quite certain what he's written. . . . Writers! There's something in Chelsea which spends a lot of time trying to get Hungarian authors out of prison. I can't think why. Writing's a job like another. The man who lives in a police state and chooses to write against it is a fool.'

'And what would you do yourself?'

'I'd write the party line. And eat.'

Rex wasn't absurdly shocked. 'You're certainly a realist.'

'I told you my mother was German.'

'And what about this writer?'

'He gummed up my naturalization.'

'But how?'

She shrugged. 'It wasn't so difficult. I told you you'd turned against us and I can't say I blame you. Applications from Hungarians get looked at pretty carefully. Amongst other things they talk to the ex-Hungarians, the ones now British, and if you're not in with the gang you don't stand much chance. And I wasn't in the clique at all. I'm not an intellectual, I'm not even what's called a liberal. I don't go to houses in Hampstead where it's smart to know Hungarians. I'm a bit of a lone wolf.'

He considered it, shaking his head. 'I shouldn't have thought that

that would be enough to fix you. The Home Office is as stuffy as the next one, but it does have the reputation of being reasonably fair. No, I shouldn't have thought that that alone would wreck your application.'

'It wasn't alone.'

He waited again whilst she drank her coffee. 'You know,' she said finally, 'we're really rather nasty. We can be charming when we try, which is mostly when it pays us, but we're shamelessly unreliable. Unscrupulous too. This writer, for instance. I was alone in London and spoke his language, so he took it for granted I'd hop into bed with him. I didn't want to, and he didn't like it. It hurt his pride, diminished him, and I could see he wouldn't forget it. I was doing quite nicely too, at nursing and, well, at nursing, whereas all he could get was an occasional talk on the Third Programme. Otherwise those Chelsea people kept him.' She sighed. 'I don't know exactly how he worked it, but he was being lionized at the time, the big boy in the precious little clan of expatriate authors. He wasn't without English friends, and some of them, in their queer world, were influential too. I don't imagine he went to the Home Office himself, but somebody did. I found that out later—never mind how.'

'And what did the somebody say?'

She stared into her coffee cup, at last said shortly, deliberately brutal: 'He said I was a whore.'

Rex Hadley was silent. The evening was dead and he knew it. He paid the bill and drove Mary Francom home. They hardly spoke at all.

And, back at Maldington, he couldn't sleep. It was shameful—an outrage! She wanted naturalization and she'd done more than most to earn it. Justice apart . . . Rex turned in his bed. He had known that it wasn't justice which was keeping him awake.

Next morning he sent for the Security Officer. He hadn't much faith in Lieutenant-Commander Rivers-Legge, but he had once worked in the Security Executive. Not a job of importance, Rex imagined—probably just training—but at least he had been at head-quarters. He might know the simpler ropes.

Rivers-Legge was a retired naval officer who took great pains that you should realize it. He walked with a quarter-deck roll; he drank pink gin and little else; his eyes were an improbable blue, his manner bluff. Rex had never been able to decide whether he was a deliberate caricature or simply an unconscious and stupid one. He was certainly very stupid. Rex didn't object to that, for his sheer stupidity was in a sense an asset. Rex wanted to ask him a question, and it was the kind of question which he would rather ask of a wholly insensitive man.

Rivers-Legge came in now and sat down. Rex looked at him undecidedly. He knew exactly how to handle Legge in theory. You fixed him with an unflinching stare and barked out the questions. Legge understood that perfectly. The trouble was that you mightn't be able to keep it up: sooner or later you smiled, not at poor Legge but at yourself. He wouldn't know it, though; he'd think you were laughing at him and that would be fatal; he'd go into his shell at once, offended and unhelpful. Finally Rex said carefully: 'Weren't you once in the Security Executive?'

'They still employ me. I sincerely trust——'

'In headquarters, I meant. I was wondering whether you could help me.'

'That's what I'm here for.'

Rex had his reservations but he went on easily. 'Then does the Executive have anything to do with applications for naturalization?'

'I'm not sure I should tell you that.' Legge was excessively stiff.

'Oh come. I put it as a question, but I dare say I know the answer. Aliens would hardly be given British nationality if there was anything specific against them, and to check on that the Home Office would make inquiries. That would mean M.I.5 and no doubt the Executive too.'

Legge wriggled in his chair. 'If you put it like that,' he said.

'That's how I put it—so would anyone else. But I wanted to ask you a proper question too.' Rex looked up suddenly, trying, but unconvincingly, for the authentic naval glare. 'When you were at headquarters, did you ever work in the department concerned?'

'I sat in it to watch things. It was part of my training.'

'It was a good department—competently run?'

'I don't think you should ask me that.'

'I am.'

Rivers-Legge wasn't liking it; he said gruffly, the fine old sea dog: 'The old man kept an eye on it himself. He more or less ran it.'

'Thank you. So that if advice were asked for it would be conscientiously given?'

'You can bet your last shirt on that. Man, woman or child.'

'Were there many women, then? Single women, I mean.'

Rivers-Legge looked at him. 'Oh yes,' he said.

Rex Hadley rose. Legge couldn't help him further, that was evident, and Rex said amiably: 'I'm very much obliged.'

Legge rolled back to his little room, frowning, muttering uneasily. He was a very stupid man but he was compulsively suspicious. For the routine of security that made him an excellent officer. Back in his office he thought, finally dialling a number on the scrambled line. A woman's voice answered him.

'Major Mortimer's office.'

'This is Commander Rivers-Legge. At Maldington, you know.'

'I'm afraid Major Mortimer's out.'

'When do you expect him?'

'I'm sorry, he left no message.'

Rivers-Legge swore unnecessarily. 'Could I speak to the old man, then?'

'Colonel Russell, you mean?' The secretary was distinctly cool. Charles Russell was sixty, but she had spent with him, more than once, evenings which had been memorable. She didn't like to hear him called old man, and she had an official problem too. She knew perfectly well that Russell's opinion of Rivers-Legge wasn't a very high one.

But Legge was saying importantly: 'It's pretty urgent.'

'Hold the line, please. I'll go and see.'

She walked down a silent corridor, and Russell sighed resignedly. He waited for the call to be put through, and when it came said formally: 'I understand it's urgent.'

'It's about Mr. Hadley, sir. He's been asking some very queer questions.'

'So?'

'About naturalization, sir. How an applicant gets it, and what part we play in the inquiries.'

'And why is that queer?'

There was a stuffy little pause, a gathering of Legge's limited abilities. At last he said portentously: 'He's interested in a woman.'

'Aren't you?'

Rivers-Legge was offended. 'Sir?'

'Let it pass.'

'Well, I was thinking. . . .' Legge wasn't at ease. When it came to the point of simple statement he was always under handicap. Simple statements needed brains. Now he said elliptically: 'We know what Rex Hadley does. If he's mixed up with a woman, a foreigner. . . .' The Lieutenant-Commander disapproved of foreigners. 'I mean, if she's an *alien*, somebody not yet naturalized——'

'She is.'

'I beg your pardon?'

Russell said precisely: 'Mr. Hadley has a woman friend and I wish them both well. I know her and approve. I vouch for her.'

'Oh.' There was an awkward little silence again. Rivers-Legge had never been quite comfortable with Colonel Charles Russell. He was the boss, Legge called him 'sir', but there was something about him, an assurance, as though he knew better. He was mostly polite, he treated you properly, but he looked at you with cool frank eyes, seeing right through you. It was decidedly embarrassing to a conscientious security officer. The man was a clever-cat: that was what he was—a clever-cat. Rivers-Legge drew a breath, at length said slowly: 'I think you might have told me, sir.'

'She's never been down to Maldington but when she does I'll brief you.'

'Thank you very much, sir.' The irony wasn't effective and Russell ignored it.

'Is there anything else, then?'

'No. That was all.'

'Well, thank you for letting me know.'

Russell put back the telephone but almost at once it rang again. This time it was Rex Hadley's office. He had started for London ten minutes ago, coming to see Russell. He was without appointment but not without hope. He'd await Colonel Russell's convenience.

Russell picked up a paper, reading it a second time. It was the report from Major Mortimer on events the night before, and Russell had again congratulated him. Mortimer hadn't risen in the Executive on his ability to organize counter-violence—plenty could do that— but on his discretion in concealing the fact of it. They had decided to conceal it from Hadley too, at any rate for the present. What was to be gained by telling him? Nothing so far as protection went. Tell a man in his middle forties that hoodlums employed by a foreign Power had intended to seize his person, to beat from him a secret. . . .

The complications were more evident than any advantage to the Executive.

Charles Russell smiled. He had met Rex Hadley but only casually. It would be particularly interesting to meet him again this morning.

Ninety minutes later Rex was shown in. Russell liked the look of him. He sat solidly but without collapse, a quiet-looking man with the air of having something in reserve. In an age of stomach ulcers, or taut tense men, Russell approved him at once. . . . But he ought to be relaxed! He didn't know, he couldn't conveniently be told, that but for the Executive he would at this moment be in hospital at best. Rex said politely: 'It's kind of you to see me.'

'Not at all. I hope it won't surprise you that I know a great deal about you, but we've only met once before, that was some time ago, and I remember I did the talking. That was a mistake. Security is nine-tenths paper, but the other tenth, knowing a man, is something I always miss.' Russell poured sherry—not quite his best, for he was sparing of his very best, but it was admirable sherry. He asked with apparent innocence, thinking of the night before: 'You drove yourself up to London?'

'In point of fact my man drove. He's a great one for coming to London. I imagine he's found a girl here.' Rex drank some wine. 'That's what I wanted to see you about.'

'Your manservant's girl friend?'

'No, my own.'

'There's some trouble with a woman?'

'No trouble at all. There's one I'd like to help, though.'

'I'm probably quite the wrong man.'

'Do you mind if I tell you?'

'They pay me to listen.'

'Then I'm friendly with a Mary Francom. That isn't her name and I don't know her real one. I doubt if it matters. She's a Hungarian— a nurse and a useful person. She wants to be naturalized and I'd like to help her.'

. . . An intelligent, a successful, engineer. And something as well, a man who would help a friend.

But Rex was repeating: 'She wants British nationality and that would come to you.'

'Just a minute. It might or it might not. It would go to the Home Office first, and if they knew nothing against your friend they'd ask for a check-up—here or with colleagues. But if they didn't like the girl, if they had something against her themselves, I'd never see the papers. I wouldn't have need to.'

'I'm afraid that's what happened in this case. Somebody in the

Hungarian clique in London took against her. He went to the Home Office or had something conveyed there. He said she was undesirable.' Rex hesitated, then said firmly: 'I believe her that that's what happened.'

'If it helps you, so do I. Implicitly. I know something about Hungarians in London.'

'But not about Miss Francom?'

Russell hated to lie: instead he said smoothly: 'If I did, then I couldn't tell you.'

'I'm sorry if I've been tactless.'

'No.'

'Then can you help me—her?'

'Frankly, I doubt it.' Russell walked to the window, staring at a pigeon on the ledge. He was fond of birds but detested pigeons. They were rodents, not things of the air, a carpet of rats in Trafalgar Square, a sea of them in the Piazza di San Marco. He made an irritable gesture uncommon with him. He had been expecting a visit from Rex Hadley, sooner or later they had been bound to meet again, but he hadn't been expecting this. Rex Hadley had fixed him. Russell would have given a great deal to be able to say that he knew Mary Francom, that she worked for him and was working now. With an interest, amongst others, in Rex Hadley himself. He shook his head impatiently. That was out of the question. And he would have liked to say he admired her. He knew her story, all of it, the Home Office fiasco too. It had infuriated him, but he knew his Home Office. It would be useless to appeal to them. Mary Francom wasn't virginal. You could put that rather differently and somebody had. The brute facts supported him. The facts! A woman alone and penniless, a vivid and vital woman.

In the world of officialdom, of Chislehurst and Croydon, that wouldn't mean a thing. There were rules and they wouldn't dare stretch them. Not even for Russell. There was public opinion. . . .

Hell.

Russell grimaced, his hands on the windowsill. The pigeon had flown, forgotten. He liked Mary Francom. She was his agent and a courageous woman. If he'd been rather younger. . . .

And Hadley was a decent man.

It was a dreadful thing to give advice since people sometimes took it. It was an uncovenanted responsibility and God knew he had enough of them. He returned to his desk slowly. Rex Hadley hadn't moved. Russell poured more sherry, drinking it rather faster than he normally drank good sherry. At last he asked deliberately: 'You want to help Mary Francom?'

'Yes.'

'Who wants British nationality?'

'She does.'

'Forgive me if I'm impertinent—I've got to ask. You like her a lot?'

'A lot.'

'You're British yourself?'

'Of course.'

'Then why don't you marry her?'

CHAPTER VII

On the other side of the Channel Jacques and Pierre had at once reported and had been disciplined just as quickly; and within an hour the story had come back to de Fleury. Victor, he was thinking, was prompt at least, but apart from that reflection he was furious. The loss of Jacques and Pierre was something he could accept—they had been useful potentially but also expendable—but Victor's action had been an insult. It was true that he had had Cohn killed without even informing his military attaché, but there had been justification for that. Military attachés were the happier, the safer too, not to be consulted in some gutter killing, but de Fleury had been sent to London with a precise and agreed plan. He had accepted the assignment gladly, since it had saved him from the probability of a considerable spell in prison. Still, he had had his instructions, the terms of his employment in a sense, and Victor had arbitrarily overridden them, indulging the crudest violence—madness. de Fleury genuinely detested violence. This wasn't some steaming colony, or a desert crust on an ocean of oil. Victor had been good in those—oh, very. This was London, a civilized capital in its queer English way, and Hadley far from some frightened native. Victor loved violence for violence had served him well. The beatings-up, the torturings, the police who arrived too late. . . .

The provinces of empire lost, the sapping, degrading wars.

Not here—not here indeed. Victor was mad to think of it; Victor, of course, was a little mad. To serve what he served he had to be.

de Fleury considered the new situation. The Security Executive had been intelligent; they hadn't wanted an open political scandal and they'd neatly avoided one. But had they told Hadley that there had been a plan to beat information out of him, a brutal scheme hatched in another country? If that were so then blackmail, even the severest forms of it, would seem small beer. But de Fleury didn't believe that Hadley would have been told. He wouldn't have told him himself, for it was an axiom of the trade that a man who needed protection was very much easier to protect if he wasn't aware of it; and everything the Executive had done, or rather had not, suggested that its policy was that the fewer people knew about last night the better.

In which case Hadley would know nothing of any attempt at violence; all Hadley would know was that de Fleury had strings on him. Very well then, he'd tighten them. Victor, head down, had come charging in and earned for his pains a smarting snub. That was how he'd see it—a rebuff from Charles Russell, a rival. But the original plan was still uncompromised, so why not proceed with it? de Fleury had never imagined that Rex would break at once, indeed he would have been astonished if he had even shown signs of it. The essence of blackmail was that it was cumulative, a weapon in a craftsman's hands. And de Fleury was a craftsman with a craftsman's pride. This was where the skill came in, the expertise and judgement. They'd sent him to London to use them, the calculated, mounting squeeze. He'd been successful before and with very tough men.

de Fleury rose, pouring himself a whisky. His forebears had been serving kings when Victor's had been peasants. Victor had come lunging in, a middle-class soldier, a violent clown. . . .

de Fleury finished his drink. He'd stick to his plan for he was certain it was a good one. He'd timed the next move carefully, plotting a curve of strength. He'd given Hadley a week and the week was almost up. So he'd hit him again and he'd strike where it hurt. Now he'd strike at his private life.

He began to check carefully, for he was thorough as well as ruthless; he reached for a file. It was a dossier on Rex Hadley and the Executive itself wouldn't have been ashamed of it. de Fleury read it through again. . . . There had been an unhappy marriage, and then, six weeks ago, divorce. Mrs. Hadley had had money and the alimony hadn't been crippling. Hadley had played the gentleman—the usual place and at one of two usual hotels. That had been six weeks ago, and at present there was only the decree *nisi*. So there'd be six more weeks before the absolute. Rex Hadley was starting life again; Rex Hadley was vulnerable.

de Fleury dialled a number. 'Is that van Omnigens?' van Omnigens were solicitors of formidable eminence, standing advisers to de Fleury's embassy. They were also, when they trusted you, rather more forthright than most. 'Mrs. Beatrix Agar, please. My name's de Fleury.'

Presently a soft voice answered him. A great many people had underestimated that gentle voice, and most had regretted the misjudgement.

'Francis?'

'Beatrix, can you dine with me? Tonight? I know it's short notice.'

'I'd love to but I've a date.' Mrs. Agar regretted her previous engagement. She chose her men friends carefully and Francis de Fleury was a favourite.

'Then tell me about your divorce law. I gather it's an anachronism.'

'Francis, you're coming on. English divorce law rests on the assumption that two people who want a divorce and could arrange one decently shouldn't be allowed it unless one of them has committed what's called a matrimonial offence.'

'You're joking.'

'I wish I were. Have you heard of the bench of bishops?'

'We tamed our own.'

'I wish I could say the same. Not that I'm not sorry for them sometimes. Twenty years ago or so they wanted to change their prayer book, the way they spoke to God in fact. And what do you think happened? Parliament wouldn't let them.'

de Fleury said cautiously: 'I'm a foreigner. This is England.'

'You're a diplomat and delicate. But it doesn't work like that when anything important comes along, divorce law, for instance—something which affects the lives of ordinary people. Then politicians listen with their ears pinned back. That's *votes*, you see, or might be, and votes are politics, not prayer books.'

'I don't think I follow.'

'I can't say I blame you. This, as you said, is England. In America, where legal cruelty means anything from having the wrong haircut to not eating breakfast they manage less outrageously, and in catholic and logical countries where the Church is still powerful divorce is quite simply impossible. But otherwise it's civil law. Here we get the worst of both worlds.'

'I don't understand it.'

'Poor Francis, poor sensible foreign Francis. I told you you couldn't have a divorce simply because both of you wanted one. That would be too easy, divorce by consent, and that's a dirty word. So if neither of you has indulged in a matrimonial offence, and probably neither has, one of you either has to commit one or else to pretend to. Mostly you simply pretend, but if it's found out that's terrible. You've cheated, tried to deceive the wise and learned judge. You won't get your decree or, if you've got a first decree, a *nisi*, it might even be rescinded. That's happened where someone's been careless or when somebody did the dirt on him.' There was a feline chuckle. 'Don't quote me, by the way. We're terribly respectable.'

'How long between the first decree and what you call the absolute?'

'Three months if it breaks your way. Francis, I know you're a bachelor. I ask no questions, but you can send him to me if you like. Not both of them—ever. Meanwhile I'll tell you something. It makes me ashamed, it makes me sweat, but you pay us very hand-somely.'

'All right then, tell me.'

'Far and away the easiest matrimonial offence to handle is straight adultery. I can't give your friend a name—my senior partners would have strokes—but I could give him an introduction who will give him an introduction who will give him another. You'll have gath-ered it's a sort of game, a shameful one. So you find your woman and take her away. She'll be a professional, of course. One of the best has three boys at prep. school and does it to pay the fees.'

'You're obliged to go to bed with her? Forgive me if I sound innocent. I'm only a poor foreigner.'

'She'd scream if you tried. You sleep on the floor and set your alarm for half-past seven. When it goes off you undress and get into bed with her. Then you ring for breakfast and, if you've chosen the right hotel, the chambermaid knows the drill.'

'So it depends on the chambermaid?'

'Where they have chambermaids.'

'And what about the hotel register?'

'That wouldn't be enough alone, not unless there was a long back history of association with the same woman. The theory of the thing is that she's simply a tart you picked up.'

'And if the servant breaks down? If she makes a mess of giving evidence?'

'If you go to the right hotel she won't.'

'But if she does?'

'It would depend on the judge's liver. And religion.'

'Suppose she were later to change her mind—resile?'

'And why should she do that?' Beatrix Agar was surprised.

'I just wanted to be sure, I——'

But Beatrix interrupted him. 'Listen, Francis, I think I've said enough. Send your friend along to me.'

'Thank you,' he said, 'I will.'

He put up the receiver, pleased. It had been much as he had

thought. He looked at Hadley's file again, confirming a place name. Then he sent for a taxi and directed it to Victoria.

He caught a train to Brighton.

Rex noticed the letter next evening for it hadn't come by post. He opened it standing and read it once quickly. Then he took it to his study.

It was quite a short letter and expressed unequivocally. The writer had been to a seaside resort called Brighton, and there he had passed a night at an hotel which was vulgarly known as the Jezebel. His breakfast had been brought to him by an Italian floor-waiter named, unremarkably, Giorgio. As Mr. Hadley might remember, the writer spoke Italian, and the floor-waiter had been delighted to talk his own language. He had in fact talked freely—very freely. He'd been concerned in a recent divorce case, and the evidence he had given had at the time amused him. Now he wasn't so amused, for the writer had had a little talk with him. He'd talked about English law, the extraordinary, the incomprehensible respect in which the English held it. The waiter had begun to wonder. Not that mere doubt was final, but the waiter was venal as well as cynical; he had a home in Italy and would like to go back there. With capital, of course. So the writer had explained to him how that capital might be forthcoming. A simple statement to the appropriate authorities. . . . As it happened Mr. Hadley's was the first case he'd appeared in: it was later, when he'd been at the Jezebel longer, when it happened again and again, when people kept approaching him. . . . His conscience wouldn't stand for it—that would be how to put it to the English. He was an innocent Italian working man, a good catholic at that. And hadn't Mr. Hadley left him rather a large tip? For Mr. Hadley, his decree not yet absolute. . . .

Well, there it was. Mr. Hadley would remember that he owed the writer certain information.

Rex read this letter with a calmness which surprised him. The shock, he thought, came later, the blank despair. For the moment he could think impersonally and he began to do so.

. . . The police or perhaps Charles Russell? Hardly. Rex held the paper against the light. It was the cheapest foolscap, and if there was a watermark he couldn't see it. The paper could have been bought at a thousand shops. The typewriting too—it would be stupid to imagine that de Fleury would have used a typewriter which could easily be traced to him. In any case, pinning the letter to de Fleury wouldn't help Rex himself. It would be awkward for de Fleury but it wouldn't remove this Giorgio. Giorgio wanted money: it wasn't important who paid him, de Fleury or a successor. Rex remembered that it was Friday, and the evening before he had been supposed to report to de Fleury. Like some cheap petty spy. Naturally he hadn't.

. . . By God, they don't waste time.

He heard himself laugh though the sound wasn't pleasant. Russell had suggested that he marry Mary Francom. Naturally the idea had occurred to him and naturally he'd hesitated. Now he wouldn't be marrying anyone; he'd be caught in holy deadlock with Irene, so clever, so articulate Irene. She'd been interested in the mystic East and in something called social service; she'd almost destroyed him. Now he'd be tied to her for years while white-fingered lawyers, frightened to soil them, fiddled and coughed and finally did nothing.

Rex walked to his office, finishing the work he'd left that morning. There was nothing important and for that he was thankful.

He went back to his ugly house much later than usual, but with his mind made up. Russell had suggested marriage with Mary Francom, and he'd thought the idea a fair one; he'd consider it, let the proposal lie; he'd do some of that unconscious cerebration Irene had been so hot for. Now he most certainly wouldn't. He mightn't be free to marry her—not now.

So that decided it—he'd do his damnedest. He knew who might help him and it wasn't Charles Russell. He didn't like asking favours, but now he'd be obliged to. They'd dismiss him of course, he'd have to leave Maldington. That would be bitter, but it was less important than his private freedom. Sir William might help him in that since he'd been through the farce himself. He might, and there was no one else.

Rex went to bed early, setting his alarm for four o'clock. It was a longish drive to Birmingham.

CHAPTER VIII

Rex Hadley slipped downstairs. It was bitterly cold. He took his car from its garage quietly, anxious not to wake George Perkins. He didn't fancy company and he wasn't going to London. He drove away slowly, warming the engine, skirting Maldington's perimeter fence. The arc lamps on their latticed towers glared savagely, throwing no shadow where they fell direct, enormous misshapen hulks at the penumbra. Under its mild native moon Maldington had been mysterious; under this inhuman light the establishment was terrifying. It looked quite deserted: Rex knew that it was not. Take a liberty and within seconds the lighting would double; switches would click ominously, completing circuits it was better not to know about; in the three little guardhouses a buzzer would hum insistently, and men would awake from sleep, and dogs. The feral thing had stirred.

And inside the wire the same. The laboratories looked abandoned, and again Rex knew better. The night shift would be working its accustomed stint—the routine, this—and there would always be Rudolf Walther. Which wouldn't be routine at all. Rudi Walther was a night bird. Other scientists didn't like him for it was possible he was a genius. More difficult to live with still, he never joined their quarrels. Rex's smile was affectionate. Project A was a gamble and nothing might emerge from it. Rex wasn't a scientist but he believed he could assess them. It was his unspoken hunch that if anything came out of Project A then Rudi would have fathered it.

Rex pointed the car north-east and, two miles from Maldington, another slipped behind him. It wasn't the Lagonda and it was a different crew, but their instructions were identical. Rex didn't see it for it was discreetly done, and he was driving deliberately, staring ahead. There had been a light fall of snow and he didn't want an accident. He had given himself ample time. Breakfast in Edgbaston was at eight o'clock sharp, and it wasn't good policy to spoil a man's breakfast, particularly when you were asking a favour of him. Rex's decision had been a simple one: he'd tell Sir Bill everything; he'd then take his medicine but he'd ask for help too.

He pulled up a little early before a formidable Victorian mansion. It made him smile again. Sir William Banner's father had lived in this alarming house, his great-grandfather had built it. A succession of Lady Banners had fought a running but inconclusive battle with the interior decorating, but none had even dared engage the architecture. There were turrets and glass verandas, and a portico which made you blink. There were also modern central heating, superlative beds and a good deal of well-trained service. It was a brandy-and-soda house. Rex looked at his watch, waiting for half-past eight; then he drove into the crescent drive and rang.

Sir William had finished breakfast but at once offered Rex some. Rex declined but accepted coffee. Sir William had plenty of time, or if he hadn't, concealed it. He stood before an open fire, his hands behind his coat-tails. It was an antiquated attitude and with most men would have been absurd. It perfectly became Sir Bill, and Rex Hadley it reassured. Sir Bill waved at a leather armchair, then stood unmoving, his bald head slightly shiny; he looked at Rex, said evenly: 'I can see you're in trouble.'

Rex began to talk quickly, omitting nothing, finally passing Sir Bill the letter. He watched his face but it didn't change. When he had finished reading Banner asked simply: 'And that's the lot?'

'I think it's about enough.'

'Ye-es.' There was a reflective pause. 'It's this divorce-thing that matters.'

'That tape could be pretty serious. For me.'

Surprisingly Sir William shook his head. 'Did you ever play Snakes and Ladders? It's a childish affair but not without its lesson. So I see this as a game of it. The threat to block your divorce—that part of what's clearly a plan—I see as Square Two. The business at Sestriere was Square One. Take a reprimand for that and then forget it. Because if we can knock this de Fleury off Square Two it isn't any good to him that he was once on Square One. He goes back to the start again, and I doubt if there can be one. That's the way blackmail goes.'

Rex thought it over. 'Then what should I do?'

'Who were your solicitors?'

Rex Hadley told him.

'I've never heard of them—not that it matters. It wouldn't help you to go back to them. I know about lawyers, and your own would be frightened stiff. They'd think first of themselves, their own position. They wouldn't lift a finger.'

'I might go to others.'

'You might, but I don't advise it.'

Rex asked again: 'Then what should I do?'

'Nothing. Go back to Maldington. I'll settle this, or try.' Sir William looked at the elaborate ormulu clock. 'Lend me that letter, please.' He walked to the door, and at it Rex said awkwardly: 'I don't know why you should help me, sir.'

'I'll give you one good reason, Rex. You've never asked a thing.'

Sir William went to his study and began to telephone. He telephoned to his office, saying he wouldn't be in. He telephoned to his solicitors, making a date for luncheon. He telephoned to Russell, arranging an appointment for three o'clock. Then he sent for his car.

At one o'clock precisely he arrived at van Omnigens and was shown with some ceremony to Beatrix Agar's room. He produced

86

with a flourish, half deprecatory half deliberate, a large bunch of roses. He had spent a good deal of time in Europe and he had remembered to take the paper off.

'Why, Sir William!'

'Stop calling me Sir William.'

Beatrix Agar was pleased. Sir William Banner was an important client, but not every eminent client brought her flowers. He was a shrewd old boy and a bit of an old charmer in his throwaway style. Moreover he spoke his mind; he said what he had to say shortly and certainly, and to a busy solicitor that was important. He told the truth and so could you.

He took her away to luncheon, glancing at the menu, raising an eyebrow. Beatrix nodded and smiled, and Sir William ordered quickly. They had eaten together before, and Banner was known for an excellent memory. When they were settled he said: 'Do you mind if we talk shop? Then a friend of mine is in the middle of a divorce suit. The usual thing. He took a woman to the Jezebel at Brighton, where he registered in his proper name. Then the floor-waiter saw them in bed next morning and was called to court to say so. There's a *nisi* but it's not yet absolute.'

'Old hat,' she said. She was thinking that this was interesting. Francis de Fleury had been asking her about divorce. Francis was a bachelor, so Francis must have a friend. Sir William Banner was already divorced—van Omnigens had handled it—and Sir William had many friends. Just possibly. . . .

Her handsome face showed nothing. Both men were clients.

Sir William dissected a trout with astonishing neatness. Beatrix Agar watched his hands. He was a stout little man but his hands were beautiful. He pushed the backbone aside and answered her.

'Old hat up to a point.' Sir Bill ate some fish. 'But my friend has an enemy, and this enemy is offering the floor-waiter what I imagine is a considerable sum to say it was a put-up job. It was, of course. Unless, that is, my friend does something for this other man.'

Beatrix Agar said sharply: 'Blackmail.'

'A good stiff sentence?'

'A five-year stretch at least. If proved.'

Sir William shook his head again. 'It wouldn't help my friend. He won't do what this other man is asking, that I'm quite sure of, but he does want his divorce.' He handed Beatrix Agar the typed and un-signed letter.

She read it twice carefully, and whistled.

'As bad as that?'

'Not quite. There's an element of bluff, of course—in blackmail there mostly is. And some rather sketchy law. It reads as though this blackmailer were well-informed and shrewd, but he isn't a practis-ing lawyer.' Beatric nodded at the letter. 'Let's take this to pieces professionally. . . . So the waiter goes to what are absurdly called the appropriate authorities and tells them he's seen this woman in bed with other men. So what? That proves she's a wicked woman, but it doesn't prove that your friend didn't commit adultery with her on the occasion the waiter said he did. He can even say he believes she's a professional co-respondent. So what again? The facts, the original evidence, haven't been shaken. I spend a good deal of time hiring counsel to stroke a judge's whiskers, and I needn't tell you that British courts are notoriously sensitive about their dignity. They don't like to be made fools of. Your blackmailer seems to know that too, but it's a knife that cuts both ways. Before a court will admit that it's been deceived it needs something pretty definite to go on. It's a serious thing to rescind a decree *nisi*.'

'You're telling me that this is bluff? You're telling me we can ride it?'

'I didn't quite say that. Because this waiter is a foreigner, an un-educated man.' Beatrix Agar leant forward. 'I'm not worried by what this blackmailer *says* that the waiter will say; I'm worried about what he *might*. If he makes any statement at all he'll be questioned by men who know their business. Here's an ill-educated Italian who went to court and swore he had seen something. If he volunteers further comment he's bound to be asked about the original occurrence. So here's a simple and frightened foreigner getting in deeper and deeper. He won't understand our legal attitudes, he'll certainly assume that any sort of questioning means that somebody's *against* him. He'll think in terms of his native police, though the police won't be in it at all. He'll start wondering what he *ought* to say, what will extract him from the mess he's landed in. He'll ask himself what do they want of me? and it could occur to him that if he simply repudiated his original story——'

'That would be serious?'

'Very.'

Sir William thought fast and silently; at last he said: 'I can see there's a risk and I don't like risks. I'd much rather play it safe.'

'You're asking for advice on that? I doubt if a lawyer should give it.'

'I'm not asking my lawyer—not now.'

'You're an understanding man.' Beatrix laughed, demolishing a meringue. She had a splendid figure but she needed to watch it; she shouldn't have been eating a meringue. 'A delicious lunch, and I've very much enjoyed it. A lunch between friends.'

Sir Bill said: 'Understood.'

'This floor-waiter then.'

'He's a wop, as you know. The bait is a place of his own in Italy— the money to set up in it.'

'Have you any idea how much?'

'How much would you think yourself? Two hundred? Three? He has considerable resources, my poor friend's enemy.'

'I'd put it rather higher to be safe. Call it five hundred.'

'I'll call it five hundred.'

'That won't be enough.'

There was a silence while both drank their coffee. Beatrix said obliquely: 'There's something called exchange control.'

'I know how to fiddle that.'

'And don't give it all at once. Scare him to begin with. Talk about lawyers but don't mention me. Then give him something generous to start with, the rest to be paid monthly over the next six months. Provided he stays in Italy.' She collected her bag and gloves. 'Would you drive me back, please? In office hours I'm a respected and respectable solicitor.'

He drove her back, asking in her room if he could use the telephone.

'Of course.'

He rang up his bank.

When he had finished she said a little wistfully: 'It must be nice to be very rich.'

'Sometimes—not often. Just occasionally you can buy things. Satisfaction, for instance, or Italian waiters. You can outbid an enemy.' For the first time that morning Sir William Banner giggled. 'Two thousand, I thought—there's no point in cheeseparing. That's three and a half million lire. It sounds better in lire.' He picked up his hat.

'You're going down to Brighton now?'

'Good heavens, no. This wouldn't be my meat at all. I'd muddle the thing for certain.' He looked at her reflectively. 'Just between ourselves again, I've an appointment at the Security Executive.'

'It's helpful to know the right people.'

He took her hand. 'I'd rather have competent friends.' His bow was old-fashioned but Beatrix approved it. 'Friends I can lunch with.'

Charles Russell had listened in total silence. When Banner had finished he said: 'You want us to help?'

'I think it's more your line than mine.'

'I'm inclined to agree.' Russell picked up a telephone. 'Ask Major Mortimer to see me, please.'

He explained to Robert Mortimer with classic brevity. 'You think we can help?'

'Of course, sir. I'll go myself.'

'You speak enough Italian?'

'I haven't quite forgotten it.'

'Good. Take my car.'

When Mortimer had gone Sir William said: 'You're a most co-operative man.'

'And you're a very generous one.'

'I like Rex Hadley and I loathe extortioners.'

Mortimer told Russell's driver to go to Brighton fast. Half an hour behind him another car would be following. It would be half an hour behind because it had made a stop. It had stopped in Lower Regent Street for an air ticket to Naples.

Francis de Fleury had never hedged his bets, but when he wasn't gambling he was careful. He had sent Smithy to Brighton. His instructions had been clear but far from onerous. Smithy needn't keep nudging Giorgio, he needn't even meet him, since if everything went to plan Giorgio wouldn't in fact be asked to do a thing. Giorgio was a threat of action, not an essential actor. Nevertheless they couldn't afford to take a chance with him: he mustn't, for instance, be permitted to change his mind. For one thing he'd accepted a substantial payment on account. So Smithy was to take a room at the Jezebel and there he was to keep an eye on Giorgio.

Smithy had nodded. It didn't sound difficult and he was fond of Brighton.

But this evening he was telephoning to de Fleury, reporting in unmistakable urgency, saying resentfully: 'That damned waiter is packing.'

'You mean he intends to leave?'

'He's given in his notice. I had to ask outright and they didn't like it.'

Francis de Fleury considered it. 'You think he's just lost his nerve? Or has somebody got at him?'

'Maybe. But he does fifteen or twenty rooms and it might be any one of them. Or even somebody outside. Should I check?'

'There's isn't time.' de Fleury thought again. 'He's actually packed his bags?'

'He has.'

'There's the evening train from Liverpool Street—the Hook of Holland, then by the Rhinegold or the Lorelei through Basle.'

Smithy looked at his watch. 'He couldn't make that.'

'Or there's a flight in the small hours direct to Naples.'

'That's much more likely.'

'Then I'll meet you at London Airport.'

'Right.'

Giorgio was waiting for the air-hostess to clear them finally. His flight to Naples had been announced, and he was sitting in a numbered bay with the other passengers. There weren't very many for it wasn't the season—a small party of tourists and an Italian or two returning to their families. Giorgio was delighted to be doing the same. He had a round little wife, a loving little wife in Naples, but he hadn't seen her for a year. That was a long time to leave a woman in the mezzogiorno.

But though he was delighted he wasn't quite at ease. It wasn't his conscience which troubled him; he knew he was breaking a promise but it was instinct which insisted that the affair had been too easy to be wholly of good omen. He touched the medal he always wore. The bishop had blessed it himself, and normally it brought immediate reassurance. But this morning, in the hollow dawn, it wasn't as potent as usual. Giorgio had cheated and knew it, and the signore who had spoken Italian so well hadn't given the impression that he would take easily to being cheated. The so-elegant signore had known the world, and there had been something about him, an authority which Giorgio had recognized but could not name. But his proposition hadn't seemed unreasonable, and certainly it had been tempting. Giorgio had pocketed a considerable retainer. But then the English signore, the military one, the gentleman who hadn't spoken Italian quite so fluently, had been even more formidable and his proposition in turn more generous. Two thousand English pounds—a fortune! For doing nothing too—simply for going home and staying there. Five hundred on account—Giorgio had it hidden about his person for he didn't trust banks—and the rest every month provided he stayed in Italy. The military signore had frightened him, but it hadn't occurred to Giorgio to mistrust him. He could recognize a man who kept a bargain.

Now he sat on his bench uneasily, fingering his medal again, waiting for he knew not what. He wasn't a courageous man—his wife had once reproached him. Giorgio hadn't resented it since it was something he accepted. *Mi manca il dono di coraggio*, and there it was.

He saw that the hostess had come back to them, her business smile affixed and frightful. The door into Customs opened and Giorgio rose.

Two men walked up to him from nowhere. One was the first signore. They stood between him and the open door. The signore said gently: 'You were thinking of leaving us?'

Giorgio was silent. He was an uneducated man and he feared irony worse than a beating.

The other said savagely: 'You dirty, double-crossing little——'

'Be quiet.' It was the signore again. He took Giorgio's arm, quietly but with authority. 'I think you'd better come with us.'

Giorgio looked round but the hostess had disappeared. The others were almost through the door.

He was alone.

'I . . . you . . . signore. . . .'

A tall man across the waiting-room rose from behind a newspaper, walking towards them quickly. Giorgio began to tremble. It was the second, the military gentleman. He bowed briefly to the first.

'Colonel de Fleury?'

'How do you know my name?'

'It isn't important. Mine is Robert Mortimer. I'm not a policeman but there are police within call. Frankly I don't want to call them—that would be awkward for both of us. But I must if you oblige me to.'

There was silence for perhaps ten seconds. Giorgio had begun to weep. de Fleury's hand fell slowly from his arm and Robert Mortimer's replaced it. He walked Giorgio to the open door, pushing him briefly through it. Somebody shut it behind him.

Robert returned to the other two, for the first time speaking to Smithy.

'You call yourself Smith?'

'That's my name.' Smithy was facing it out.

'It wasn't the name in your last conviction, nor in any of the others. I wouldn't risk another one. I'd take a good long holiday if I were you. And a change of employment.'

'And if I don't?'

'I told you I wasn't a policeman but I've excellent friends in the police. There was the matter of that jeweller in Prince's Street. Nobody's saying you did him yet but nobody's sure you didn't.'

The man they called Smithy thought it over. 'Okay,' he said. 'You win.'

He walked away decidedly, and Mortimer turned to de Fleury.

'Naturally you're more difficult.'

'I am?' de Fleury was entirely calm. He had lost a fortune gambling but not because his face betrayed him.

Robert Mortimer was as cool. 'You are and you aren't. Your principle strength is that we don't want a scandal. That gives you rope but it isn't unlimited.' Mortimer hesitated, then said deliberately: 'Do me a favour, will you? Don't stretch the rope too far. Watch it, I beg you. All of you.'

CHAPTER IX

de Fleury drove back to his flat in the bitter knowledge of both failure and crisis. The failure had been sharp and personal: the Security Executive had overreached him, and that the overreaching had been very much in the English manner, undramatic and almost casual, didn't alter the brute fact of its achievement. de Fleury was too experienced to deceive himself: if the Executive had discovered about Giorgio it wasn't conceivable that it didn't also know about Hadley's indiscretion at Sestriere. But Hadley had been left at Maldington, therefore the Executive both knew and had condoned. Which meant that it felt perfectly safe with Hadley, which meant in turn that it wasn't afraid of any move by de Fleury against him. de Fleury hadn't heard Sir William's homely metaphor of Snakes and Ladders, but if he had he would wryly have agreed with it. Blackmail wasn't something which could be stopped, then started again from scratch. Call one card and you called the hand. Rex Hadley was in the clear.

de Fleury sighed. He had in his flat a tape which he was rather proud of. He'd keep it as a souvenir, but he must accept that it was useless.

That was the failure, galling enough, but he recognized too a personal crisis. Victor would want his money's worth: they wouldn't let him off. He'd been chosen for his connections, the social graces, background. And for their knowledge that he'd betrayed it. His wartime commission, discreetly revived, inflated into colonel—that hadn't been done to oblige him. They'd done it because they *had* him; they'd saved him from prison and now he was their creature. His plan had failed but they'd have their own, and inescapably they'd involve him. Violence, he thought—brutal, degrading violence. The world he'd been born to was almost gone. On one side the rats, the Julian Cohns, nibbled at it ceaselessly: on the other the Victors, believing that they were paladins, utterly debased the values they thought to save. The beatings-up, the torturings, the police who arrived too late. . . . And now he worked for Victor, if that were a legitimate word for it. Alas, he could think of others.

He said aloud, not knowing it: 'Dear God, I've come pretty low.'

He went into his flat. It was five in the morning, too late to telephone Mary Francom, but he would have given much for her company. She had been irritating recently, out too often when he rang her, and there had been that ridiculous scene she had made him ten days ago. Nevertheless his first thought in trouble had been to send for her. Francis de Fleury frowned. Sometime, not now, he must think about Mary Francom. It would be excessively awkward if he'd fallen for her.

He made himself coffee. Inevitably it was Victor's move again. Jacques and Pierre and Smithy were accounted for, so in a day or two a stranger would be calling on him. He might be polite or again he might not, for this time he'd be somebody pretty senior in Victor's detestable organization. So the stranger would call, and formally he'd put himself under the military attaché's instructions. But he'd have received his own already. He might listen to suggestion, matters of detail, but he wouldn't change his plan. He'd neither wish nor dare to.

And he'd want de Fleury's help; he could in fact demand it.

Francis de Fleury shrugged. He'd have to wait and it wouldn't be agreeable.

Later that morning Rex was talking to Rudi Walther at Malding-ton. Rex hadn't always liked him but had learnt to. Rudi was a German and proud of it, indeed rather pointedly Teutonic, since there had been people in England who had imagined that it would be easier for Rudi if they pretended he was an Austrian. Their motives had been generous but to Rudi infuriating. Rudi detested Austrians. They had been happy enough to be Germans while everything was going well, but as soon as the tide turned, presto, they begged to differ. Anyone would think there hadn't been half a million people in the streets of Vienna shouting their heads off for the Anschluss. And politics apart, they were a second-class lot, the heirs of an empire which had never quite come off. And that shock-ing schlumperei. . . .

So that the amiable belief that Rudi would feel happier in England if his hosts assumed he was an Austrian had produced in him a Teutonism much more noticeable than if he had been quietly accepted as a German. He wasn't a Prussian but he clicked and bowed stiffly; he affected an eyeglass which he was always dropping; he clipped his hair, but the roll of fat at the back of the neck had been beyond him, for he was tall and spare and naturally elegant.

Now he came into Rex's room, bowing, dropping the eyeglass and for once catching it. He sat down when invited to and lit a panatella. Rex had declined. Rudi said deliberately: 'I don't say we've got it—not the big bang—but I do say we know the road to it. I mean that if we ever succeed I think I see how we'll do so. There's a very long way to go, though.'

'Then how can I help?'

'You're a very good engineer and I'm a physicist. We're playing with temperatures near absolute zero.'

'Don't tell me you want me to beat it.'

'I ask nothing so stupid. It's a matter of fractions of a degree.' Rudi knocked some ash off the panatella. 'I can give you no assur-ance, far less a promise, but I can give you the evidence. And the evidence tells us that the lower we go the livelier becomes the catalyst.' Rudi smiled politely. 'Temperatures,' he said, 'are engineering.'

'So is the law of diminishing returns. You know about our power-load.'

'Yes. I know we don't make our own—we couldn't. It comes in from the grid on the pylons. We've three lines at present but there's room for four.'

'You want a few more kilowatts?'

'And your skill to use them.'

'I'll go after it at once.' Rex rubbed his chin. 'Could you call this the critical experiment?'

Rudi said cautiously: 'It's not a phrase I like. You might.'

'Then shouldn't we report it?'

'No.' Rudi had answered unhesitatingly; he rose unexpectedly, leaning his thin body against the wall, his pale eyes still on Rex's. 'There is a theory that in a totalitarian state a scientist cannot work freely. It is mistaken.' Rudi's English was almost accentless, but in moments of emphasis his speech held the tang of an alien formality. 'It is an error,' he repeated. 'For geneticists, possibly, but not for a physicist. You can tell a geneticist the results which will fit your political opinions, and you can advise him to work accordingly. If he is wise he does so. But you cannot do that to a physicist because a physicist's work can be verified much more quickly. His masters will ask him for *things*.'

'As are ours.'

'You do not quite follow me. There are well-meaning if muddled people who suppose that in a fascist or communist state a physicist's mind cannot work freely. I have tried to explain that that is not so. A physicist's mind is *necessarily* free. But not his body.'

'Oh come. We——'

'I beg you to listen. There is security at Maldington, we both know that, but at the moment it is tolerable. But go to our masters, use a phrase like critical experiment, and what do you suppose will happen? The clamps will come down at once. You have servants,

98

haven't you?—a couple. In a matter of days they will give you notice and others will replace them. You are English and underestimate your own security. It may be that I do too. And do you suppose that you will be allowed to spend weekends in London, or I in my senior common room?'

'Still——'

Rudi sat down again. 'There is no still. I didn't escape to England to use my brains—those I could use in Dresden. I came here for the little things, not intellectual freedom, the great big meaningless words, but to go where I liked and when, to know that my caddie was just a caddie. Inside this wire there will be agents—spies. That is proper and fair. But I can go where I like still, and that I value greatly. You shall not take it from me.'

'You may lose it in any case if Project A succeeds.'

'Yes—for a time. That I have accepted, for I have a debt as a guest and I mean to repay it. Moreover the time will be limited. But I will not accept that you shackle me now.' Rudi smiled his gentle smile. 'Prematurely, I assure you. We've a long way to go still.'

Rex thought it over, asking at last: 'I may call that a threat?'

Rudi Walther shrugged. 'There would always be work for me at Cambridge.'

'I think you're more useful here. On any terms.'

Rudi rose again easily. 'Then we may hope for a few more kilowatts.' He bowed and left, and Rex whistled softly. Rudi Walther had acquired an almost English talent for understatement.

Rex telephoned to London. . . . Yes, they would start on a new line at once. Since it was for Maldington. . . .

Mary Francom knew that a proposal of marriage was a serious matter and that Rex had been serious when he had made one. But he hadn't expected her to ask time to consider it, and she saw she had surprised him. He wasn't a conceited man, but he must know that materially he had everything to offer her—a home, a respectable income, the security of settled nationality. She had pointed out that they must wait, in any case, a month till his decree was absolute. He had agreed without fuss—reason was wholly with her and he was a reasonable man—but she knew she had puzzled him.

She hadn't been playing hard to get: there was something she must be sure of. She was a scrupulous woman and it was her scruples which had deterred her. They had been scruples for the future, not the past. de Fleury had been right in deciding that the Executive would say nothing to Rex about any physical attempt against him, since it was indeed an axiom that protection was both easier and more effective if the person being protected were ignorant that it was happening. But it was equally an axiom that a reliable agent shouldn't be asked to work in the dark. Mary had been told everything, the affair of Giorgio included, and the implications had been discussed with her. One of them was that de Fleury himself was no longer dangerous. She was at liberty to disengage herself. Not too abruptly—that would look suspicious—but she was free to leave him if she wished to.

Mary had said she did, and why; and over his unquestionably best sherry Charles Russell had congratulated her, waving aside as detail the fact that she wasn't yet officially engaged. He had had the air of an amiable father after a successful piece of matchmaking. Mary had thought it strange but it had touched her.

But the future? she had asked—the possibility of further violence? Russell hadn't denied that it existed, but that was a matter for the Executive. Looking solemn he had made her an unaccustomed little speech. He could well understand her question, but she would permit him to point out that one attempt had already been defeated. One mustn't relax and the Executive wouldn't, but forewarning was half the battle. And for the fiancé of an employee the Executive would regard itself as something more than officially committed. Miss Francom must accept his assurances. . . .

She had done so happily enough, for she had a high opinion of the Executive's competence. What worried her was something more feminine, a certain reservation about its logic. Russell had spelt out to her the position as he saw it: the attempt to blackmail Hadley through his marriage, the threat to his divorce, had failed; therefore blackmail had failed totally. There could be no going back to anything in the past. de Fleury had a tape still. Much good might it do him to play it since it couldn't do harm to Hadley.

Mary had listened carefully, nodding agreement. But she hadn't quite agreed. It had been unimpeachable masculine logic, but inescapably it had been male. Mary instinctively mistrusted it. The tape *might* be used again, though perhaps not directly. Experience had taught her scepticism and now she applied it. . . . Rex was quite safe from blackmail—yes; but there were other things than blackmail. There were for instance men, and not all of them were honourable. Rex for the moment was needed, but suppose they succeeded in this Project A? It was one thing to stand by a man in crisis, another to sink him quietly when his crisis—your crisis too—was over. Sir William Banner sounded reliable, Rex was always praising him, but she herself had never met him, and men made absurd mistakes with other men. And the Executive at bottom were officials. They were people you could trust but their masters were politicians. Circumstances changed, a pack could be dealt again, and it was always a great deal safer without a joker.

Without, in fact, that tape.

Mary had left Charles Russell, slipping back to the nursing home, her mind made up. Rex had offered her security, though it would have been very unlike him to have mentioned it. She didn't mean to risk it, nor, for that matter, his. Besides, she had her private pride. She had once told Rex Hadley that she was a middle-class woman, and she wasn't ashamed of her standards. A woman should bring more to marriage than her body. She had saved a good deal, more, she imagined, than Rex would guess, and that could be her dowry. But she needed more than a dowry. Rex's proposal had been made with a quiet formality more effective than conscious chivalry. The past was expunged in a single but final silence. Englishmen! They were courteous, easy to suspect of something near indifference, all the goods in the shop window. And when you got inside the shop it wasn't a shop at all. Rex had been generous and she'd like to be the same; she'd like to give him a really good wedding present.

That tape would make a beauty.

CHAPTER X

The pilot of the single-engined military aircraft had very precise instructions and some beautiful cameras. His instructions were that he should get into trouble on a routine patrol over the Channel. He wasn't to try to master a failing engine, indeed he was to radio to the nearest military airfield, which would happen to be in England, seeking permission to make an emergency landing; he was even to be seen attempting it. At the last minute his engine would mysteriously come in again and he would find that he could stagger back to base. His superiors would see to the rest. They would apologize handsomely to their esteemed English colleagues: the pilot had been inexperienced and had been suitably reprimanded; the whole affair was most regrettable, an unnecessary alarm of the sort which was alas unavoidable with a pilot on his first flight in a high-performance aircraft of the type in question. It was particularly unfortunate that it seemed possible that the aircraft had crossed an English prohibited area.

Now Victor was looking at the excellent air photographs which the automatic cameras had brought back. An expert was interpreting them. 'No extension to Maldington,' he was saying. 'No further building. There's been a change, though.'

'What change?'

The expert told him.

'And what do you make of that?'

The expert shrugged. 'You should ask an engineer, sir. I can only report the facts. Maldington has been working for some time, and it's been working on three power lines. Now there are clearly four.' He put a pointer on one of the photographs. 'Perfectly clear—no doubt of it. It would have been simple to put in four originally, so perhaps they didn't need them. The inference would be that now they do. And from that you could infer again, and plenty. But I leave that to you, sir.'

Victor said coolly: 'You may,' dismissing him. He smoked most of a black cheroot before he picked up the telephone. He asked for an urgent interview with the tall man. He sought of him neither advice nor help, but he had decided to report a recent failure. Victor didn't always report his successes but he sometimes reported his failures; he thought nothing of the tall man's praise but his anger could be useful. When the tall man was angry he would authorize almost anything. Victor smiled grimly. What he was considering needed a top authority.

Presently the telephone rang back. The earliest appointment possible, and this was a favour, would be at eleven o'clock that evening. Victor at once confirmed it. He looked at his watch—eight hours. He could use eight hours.

He sent for the man he trusted best and they began to talk quietly. The other said doubtfully: 'I dare say it's on in theory. That is, as a staff exercise.'

'It's on all right.'

'And suppose we're captured?'

'That mustn't happen.'

Francis de Fleury had answered the doorbell. He wasn't easily surprised but now he was astonished. He had been expecting a visitor, probably some thug, but he hadn't been expecting this one. He was looking at Victor himself.

Victor came in and they went into the living-room. He accepted a drink but hardly touched it. For the moment he was polite and even formal. 'I expect you know why I'm here,' he said.

'I'm rather afraid I do.'

Victor's expression did not change. He sat quite still, very sure of himself, a heavily-built man in his sixties. His grey hair was cut *en brosse* and an empty arm sleeve, neatly folded, was pinned against his coat. He carried his head on shoulders which were powerful still, a little forward, like a wicked old bull, de Fleury thought, an animal. A formidable animal. He said at length: 'Naturally we have a plan.' He began to explain it and de Fleury listened carefully. He was indeed obliged to. Victor was from the south-west coast and years of service hadn't civilized his accent. To Francis de Fleury his speech was almost a foreign language.

... A savage, almost an alien, speaking too carefully, a dangerous and dedicated man. Perhaps they were the same.

When he had finished de Fleury said: 'Absurd.'

'You wish to suggest some local modification?' The manner was less formal now, verging on open arrogance.

'I wish to suggest that we start from the beginning. There isn't the slightest evidence of a genuine breakthrough at Maldington.'

'You may be right. But there is evidence of progress—knowledge. We have scientists ourselves, and given the proper lead——'

'But the risk, man.'

Victor didn't answer. He lit one of his own cigarettes. de Fleury hadn't used them for years. The smell was nostalgic but the smoke made him cough. When he had recovered he said again: 'The risks.'

'I have calculated the risks.'

'And I think you have done the sum wrong. Reflect. Suppose you succeed, and I don't think you will. Diplomatic relations, already delicate, will drop to zero.'

Victor said indifferently: 'Nothing could be proved if we succeed.' It was evident that a fluttering in the international dovecotes wouldn't be a matter to disturb him.

'And if you fail?'

'If we fail it will be embarrassing.' Victor unexpectedly stood up, adding in open menace now: 'For all of us.'

'What you mean is that you've strings on me.' de Fleury wasn't a coward and now he was angry. 'We're in this together and you want my help.'

'Nothing active, I assure you. Your distaste for action is well known.' Now Victor wasn't hiding his contempt. 'But there are details which you could confirm for us, timings and movements. They are not essential—do not delude yourself that you can block this plan—but equally they would be useful.'

de Fleury had been fighting temper, now he lost it. 'I'll see you in hell, the lot of you. If you come through this affair without a killing you'll be lucky. I've killed myself but I'm not an assassin.'

'Colonel de Fleury, you are in a most delicate situation. You have failed yourself and I know everything about you. Now you are withholding co-operation.'

'Co-operation—balls! Co-operation with a gang of murderers.'

'No. With me.'

'You're going on this thing yourself?'

'I am not. I shall be out of this country before it even starts. I came here to check it.'

de Fleury opened his mouth but shut it again. He had been about to make the obvious retort but his eye had caught Victor's sleeve. He had been within distance of a gaucherie and it annoyed him. He walked to the door and held it. As Victor went past him he asked: 'And for when is this idiot plan?'

'Tonight.'

In his room at the Executive Russell was saying to Robert Mortimer: 'I'm not too happy.'

'But it's all in the open now, sir.'

'*They're* in the open—we're not. One of the disadvantages of a free society is that you can't just tell people to do things. Something

106

is happening at Maldington, and our job would be a great deal easier if we could tell everybody of importance there simply to stay put. But go to the average scientist, suggest that he restrict his personal movements, and he'll go screaming to his professional association with some hair-raising story about the wicked Executive playing Senator McCarthy. There'd be a question in Parliament before you could say knife. They'd all go crying to mother, every man jack of them. All except Rudi Walther, who wouldn't run crying to anyone. He'd quietly go back to Cambridge.'

'I agree, sir—I know the form. But as far as Hadley is concerned there's been a known attempt against him. Known, that is, to us. We could tell him that in confidence; we could tell him that he's an object of some interest. That puts it mildly.'

'We could, but we decided not to. Would it help you if we changed our mind?'

'Not significantly. Hadley is only one of several, and I don't think we could accept a position where everybody of importance at Maldington was sweating on the possibility that Victor might make a violent pass at him. There's Doctor Walther, for example. His reputation is international.'

'So international that he gets asked to white tie banquets.'

'I know, sir. Tonight. With Hadley.'

Russell asked briefly: 'Then what are your arrangements?'

'Perkins will be with them; Perkins is a limpet. And there's a standing patrol round Maldington.'

'The patrol has been compromised.'

'You mean Victor knows of it?'

Charles Russell nodded.

'True. But he also knows it's armed. It shoots.'

Russell began to doodle on his pad. It was something he didn't do often, and Mortimer watched him anxiously. Without looking up Russell said: 'If a real breakthrough comes there'll have to be restrictions for a time. That we could wear and will, but just for the moment we're getting the worst of both worlds. Within the limits of the problem set us I think you've done everything possible, but I don't pretend I'm easy in my mind. We've a reliable toughie who sticks close to Hadley, and there's an armed patrol in the country besides the normal guards at Maldington. It sounds all right, it *is* all right against any ordinary villainy, for instance against another attempt at getting information by a quick beating-up. But there's one thing that can't be stopped—an operation of open war in peacetime. That cracks any security possible.'

'I'm not quite sure what you're suggesting, sir.'

'Unfortunately nor am I. I only wish I were.' Charles Russell stopped doodling; he said in the voice which Mortimer heard seldom: 'Victor—I hate his guts.'

Mary had been obliged to plan carefully for a final evening with de Fleury. She was determined that it should in fact be final. There were obvious reasons, Francis the most immediate, and there was personal inclination too. She had been told she might disengage herself, and that had been welcome since, Rex apart, there had been something about Francis lately, a manner which had begun to trouble her. She hadn't thought much about it for she wasn't being paid to. Francis de Fleury had been part of a job: it wasn't her business to analyse his emotions. The fact remained that recently he'd been extremely insistent. When she'd finally telephoned accepting for this evening she had heard him catch his breath, and later he had sent a car for her. Francis had always been considerate, but he'd never done that before.

. . . This evening—it had to be this evening. Rex was at some boiled shirt dinner; Rex wouldn't ring her.

Mary took the car to Cheyne Walk. She carried no arms for she had other weapons.

She spent the next hours using them, not despising herself for she was too much a realist, but unaffectedly happy that this was finality. She was charming to de Fleury since he was still an assignment. It wouldn't do to botch it, nor her private plan. de Fleury himself was drinking more than usual, and Mary didn't try to stop him. He was under some strain but she didn't question him. She watched the cigarettes he couldn't finish, and she watched his glass. Brandy it was, and so much the better. The harder he slept the easier her task would be.

By three o'clock she judged he was sound asleep, not drunk, but he had brought the bottle with him. She slipped from the warm bed silently, not bothering with a dressing-gown. She knew where he kept the tape. In the living-room she opened the bureau quietly, pulling at an inside drawer.

It was there and she put her hand out.

The light went on shatteringly and Mary swung. de Fleury was at the door. He was holding a gun. For a long time he stared at the tape. At last he said: 'Please put that down.'

She put it down.

'Now go and get dressed. No tricks.'

When she returned he was sitting on the sofa, covering the door along the corridor. He nodded at a chair and, when she sat down, put the gun on a table beside him.

'And now?' he asked.

She didn't answer.

With a gesture she was quite unready for he dropped his head in his hands. 'Oh, God,' he said, 'dear God.'

Mary was a warm-hearted woman and she said involuntarily: 'Francis. . . .'

His head came up slowly, his face a mask of grief. 'Take it,' he said, 'take it. It isn't any good to me.'

'But I don't understand.'

'You're an agent—just an agent.'

'Aren't you one too?'

'Of course I am. I'm an agent but I'm also a man. A man you've betrayed.'

She didn't believe her ears. '*Betrayed* you?'

'Yes. I was going to marry you.'

She stared at him, wide-eyed but not incredulous. Francis de Fleury was presently a spy, and privately he was a rogue, but it didn't occur to her that he would lie. She managed to say lightly: 'Nonsense.'

'You think so?' There was a hint of asperity and Mary welcomed it. Francis was recovering and that was more comfortable. 'You think so?' he said again. 'In any case I'm finished—through.'

'I guessed you were in trouble.'

'I was and I still am.' His hands moved unexpectedly and Mary watched them. They didn't go near the gun. 'What do you know about me? What did they tell you?'

'You're not like the men you work for. You're a man of position who lost his money gambling. Then you were a blackmailer, I gather a successful one. Then they sent you to England.'

'You know most things about me.'

'You said I was an agent. I've been briefed.'

'Not quite completely. I d like you to know it all. After I lost my patrimony I found work. It was a very good job for I had plenty of contacts. But I failed. I had honour of a sort but I could never be simply honest. Then I preyed on the world I told myself had destroyed me, the new rich men, the politicians much crookeder than I was. It was surprisingly easy and I became rather good at it. Then I overreached myself and suddenly it wasn't easy. I might have gone to jail, I nearly did. Then the men you were talking about stepped in —I was just what they wanted. I had the background, languages, a certain skill, and above all things they *held* me. I would do what they told me. I must.

Mary said softly: 'Francis, I'm very sorry.' Instinctively she had been talking for time, to calm him, a man with a gun, and now she wasn't. She was a woman and fascinated. There was a word for the Francis de Fleurys but in England people sniggered if you used it. Which was a tiresome snobbery reversed. This was one sort of man, an unhappy man, a proud one, a survival.

'Francis, why don't you quit? They've got you while you work for them, but why don't you simply run—ask for asylum . . . anything . . . I don't know. But *run*.'

He dropped his head again and she heard him groan. When he raised it his face was ravaged. 'I'm afraid to,' he said. 'Not physically —no. They'd probably go after me—I know too much, they'd have to—but it isn't that and I'd like you to believe it.'

'I do.' It was the truth.

'But it's something at least as shameful. I need money as some men need drink. It's in my blood.'

She said on a note of faint contempt: 'The trouble with you, you're an aristocrat.'

'So? But they're an unpredictable lot.'

Mary laughed.

She knew at once that she had blundered. The ravaged face was hard again. de Fleury said icily: 'I'm sorry if I've bored you. To return to our business.'

He had picked up the gun again and Mary watched it. She wasn't yet frightened, simply unbelieving.

'If you mean about the tape——'

'I do not. The tape is unimportant in itself. What matters is that you were stealing it.'

'I'm an agent like you.'

He said with a shocking dignity: 'You're the woman I loved. You betrayed me.'

Mary was frightened now. She was utterly lost. She was a practical woman with a hard life behind her. This was a language she neither spoke nor wished to. de Fleury wasn't drunk but nor was he quite sober. The threshold was lowered, and something had walked over it, something outside experience. Mary said what first came to her, urgently and in fear: 'What century are you living in?'

It didn't touch him. 'Several too late, perhaps.' For a second he lowered the gun.

. . . Jump for it? She couldn't. She'd been shot at before and she'd been terrified. But that had been real. The men behind the guns had motive, evil perhaps but rational. This was a lunatic dream.

She stared at de Fleury, frozen. His face was a death's-head now.

. . . But he was as horrified as she was, caught in some dreadful pride, a nightmare. She saw his lips move soundlessly, straining to catch his speech. It might have been a prayer.

'Francis. . . .'

The gun came up.

CHAPTER XI

Thinking it over later Robert Mortimer would have agreed with Russell that an operation of war in peacetime was something which couldn't be stopped short of counter-measures impossible in a civilized country not at war. When its enemy was prepared to use unlimited explosives, helicopters and para-military personnel, the Security Executive was playing away from home. Short of a platoon of infantry, a troop of tanks, the attempt at least could hardly have been prevented. The man-snatch had been superbly planned.

The crew of the patrol car would also have agreed if they had ever had time to do so. But they did not. They were cruising quietly, not in the old Lagonda but in a nondescript grey saloon. Though Rex didn't know it Perkins' suitcase in the boot of the Rapier was sending out a tracker-wave, and the crew of the grey saloon knew that it was a mile and a half behind them. They were alert but they weren't expecting to die.

The extravagantly powerful anti-tank mine blew the saloon to matchwood. Five men sprang from nowhere. They were wearing the camouflage uniform of parachutists but without badges of rank or numerals. They dragged into the ditch the worst of the wreckage and was was left of the crew of three. It wasn't very much. Then they waited again.

A mile and a half behind George Perkins was driving the Rapier. Rudi and Rex Hadley were in the back. They had heard a sharp explosion, but in the neighbourhood of Maldington explosions weren't uncommon. Rudi had stirred to say: 'I expect that's Carrington. That man has a passion for noise, but unhappily it's never the right one.'

He had settled again to sleep it off. Rudi didn't care for formal dinners but had relieved the occasion with considerable draughts of his native Niersteiner. He didn't normally sleep much before four in the morning, but now he was nodding. Rex was awake, reflecting that the evening had been an odd one. They had been dining with the top brass of the nuclear world, and it tickled a sharp sense of irony that if Project A succeeded many of these eminent administrators would be out of a job. Rex smiled, correcting himself. But that simply wasn't true. They were solidly of the Establishment, and if one job fell to pieces under them they would slide into another so smoothly as to be unnoticeable. There was always a committee for a good committee man.

He felt the car brake suddenly, accelerate again.

'What was that?'

'I'm sorry, sir. I thought I saw something.'

George Perkins had in fact seen something. A man had been standing in the middle of the road, waving a lamp at him, and on a reflex George had braked. Then, thinking now, he had put his foot down. The man had jumped, but only just, and Perkins drove on quickly, very awake indeed. He didn't believe that that would be the end of it. He turned on the spotlight.

Fifty yards further the beam picked them up, two barriers of steel and wire, upended at each road-side. They went down together, perfectly timed, and now George braked seriously. He knew he couldn't crash them for he'd seen such things before. They were light enough to be manhandled but they were very well designed. They were strong enough to hold an armoured-car.

George stopped with a yard to spare and two bricks broke the window. The muzzles of machine pistols followed them. There was a little knot of men, eight of them, or ten, in something which looked like uniforms. Rudi was swearing in German. Somebody said in English: 'Out.'

They all got out.

'Get that wire away, and fast. Maurice, you take the car.'

Two men ran to the barriers, moving them with surprising ease. A third man climbed into the Rapier, driving it along the road, then backing it away from it. He knew precisely where to back. The other two men returned.

'Search them.'

They found George Perkins' gun.

'Now move. All three of you.'

They walked into a little wood at gunpoint. A hundred yards ahead was the perimeter fence—seventy yards of thinnish wood, then thirty of cleared ground, finally the wire itself. The arc lamps on their towers threw a merciless light on the clearing, but at the edge of the thicket the English-speaking voice said: 'Halt.'

They stopped in a huddle, out of the light and silent. The men in uniforms seemed to be listening. One of them muttered in a language which wasn't English, and the leader said sharply: 'They'll come all right, don't fear.' He turned to his prisoners. 'Smoke if you must but keep under cover.'

George Perkins suddenly broke for it, running towards the fence. It was quite unexpected, senseless, and for an instant nobody moved. Then there was a single shot, expert and silenced. George Perkins fell half-way across the clearing. He lay quite still.

Rudi Walther began to swear again, but not in German. He swore in a febrile rage, wholly untypical; he stamped his feet and waved his arms; he frothed and he wept. It was an exhibition, decidedly diverting in its way.

They were diverted. They gathered around him, laughing contemptuously.

George had begun to crawl towards the fence.

Somebody, above the laughter, said:

'Should I quieten this kraut?'

'They're not to be hurt. That will come later.'

Somebody else said: 'God in heaven.' He was looking towards the fence, staring at Perkins, not believing. George had reached the wire; he was pulling himself upright by his hands, his legs hanging useless. Somehow he was almost upright now, his right arm reaching.

There was another shot and George's body shuddered. But his arm went on, above the chain-wire, up to the four strands of barbed, one, two, the third, the last. . . .

This time it was a burst, murderous and final. What was left of George Perkins fell.

Rudi Walther reverted to German; miraculously he was himself again. 'Sons of abortioners. Swine.'

The man behind him clubbed him.

Overhead there was the unmistakable clatter of a helicopter, then another.

Somebody fired a green.

In the three little guardhouses buzzers were humming insistently, and men awoke from sleep, and dogs. A man with a fine moustache, buckling his holster, looked at an electric indicator. 'Section Q, mile zero-zero-four. We're much the nearest. Run.'

They ran into the freezing night, four men, three dogs. The men on their rubber soles were quiet, the Alsatians utterly silent. They ran to heel, head down, their elegant sterns waving. The men ran hard for a minute, then they stopped. They slipped into the cover of the thicket, and the leader said softly: 'Do you see what I see?'

'I *think* I do. There's a helicopter coming in and I'm sure I can hear another. I see a stiff against the wire. I see men in what might be uniform, and armed. They're carrying one man and hustling another. It looks like a snatch.'

'Can you recognize who they've got?'

'I can't.'

'*I* can.' The leader thought for five seconds, then made his decision. 'Too risky to fire till they break. When they do, shoot to kill.' He snapped his fingers gently twice. The dogs rose from their haunches, their pink tongues lolling. The leader pointed; said a single word.

The dogs were away in silence.

The first man saw nothing. He lay on his side, his life pulsing out of him from what had been his throat. A second had time to fire but missed. He never missed again. A third drew a knife but the Alsatian knew that one. There was a shocking scream. He fell on his back, feebly defending himself. A fourth shot the bitch as she stood over him. The group hesitated; broke; ran for the thicket.

From its edge there was a lick of wicked flame. The man behind the light machine-gun had had time to get his bipod down and he was shooting quite brilliantly. He'd had orders to kill and he was killing with pleasure. He'd seen a dead bitch and he'd loved her.

It was over in four savage bursts. The gunner had wasted none of them. From somewhere in the thicket a red rocket plumed up lazily.

The helicopters sheered away.

Rex picked himself up unsteadily. A man with a large moustache was walking towards him. . . . Hell, he was going to salute! Rex mustn't laugh and he wanted to laugh badly. Laughing might help him.

'Are you all right, sir?'

'I think so. But Doctor Walther. . . .'

They turned Rudi Walther over, and Moustache felt him expertly. 'Unconscious—knocked cold. But he isn't wounded.' He nodded towards the fence. 'Luckier than that one. That's your servant if I'm not mistaken, sir.'

It was. He knew about the alarm wire.'

'*He* triggered us?'

'He did.'

'And who are the other stiffs?'

'I heard them speaking—it isn't a guess.'

Moustache said doubtfully: 'There's rather a lot to explain, sir. Helicopters, foreigners trying to snatch you——'

'There certainly is but it must wait till tomorrow. Report everything to Commander Legge. Ask him to pass it on. I'll be back to fill in detail by midday.'

Moustache didn't like it; he asked, more doubtful than ever: 'And where are you going now, sir?'

'I'm driving back to London.'

'Then I'll send for a driver.'

'No.'

Moustache pulled it thoughtfully. 'But are you fit to drive, sir?'

Rex Hadley shrugged.

He found his car undamaged and started for London, conscious that he wasn't thinking clearly. He did not care. He had heard the speech of the men in uniform and the language had been de Fleury's. de Fleury was a blackmailer but his compatriots were murderers, and de Fleury was Mary's friend, or had been. That was enough. There wasn't a valid reason why she should now be in danger, but this wasn't the moment for careful logic. Rex would have admitted that he was incapable of reasoning: what drove him was instinct. George Perkins had been shot in two, there had been foreigners in a sort of uniform, machine-guns and helicopters, dogs. . . . Quite an evening. Rex hadn't seen its like for eighteen years. So at least he must warn Mary. Somehow de Fleury had been part of this appalling night. Never mind how or why—he'd work it out later. There was plenty to work out later. Just for the moment there were Francis de Fleury, Mary, a connection, danger. . . .

Rex Hadley, severely shocked, could smell it. He looked at the speedometer, forcing himself to slow. He wouldn't warn Mary dead.

He pulled up at the nursing home, ringing the night bell. He had to ring three times, shifting his feet, cursing in a tension which he recognized but held him helpless. Presently an elderly woman opened.

'I want to see Miss Francom.'

The elderly nurse was outraged. She looked Rex up and down; finally she said acidly:

'It's three in the morning.'

'I'm her fiancé.'

'I don't care who you are. You ought to be ashamed of yourself.'

It occurred to Rex that this elderly woman in the fussy dressing-gown would probably think him drunk, and in a sense she would be right. He pulled himself together with an effort which was physical. Trying to speak normally he said: 'I'm very sorry to have knocked you up, but something urgent has happened. If I write a message for Miss Francom will you take it to her?'

The nurse looked at Rex again. She had thought him drunk but now she did not. She knew shock when she saw it, and she saw it as a nurse. Something *had* happened. It was probably nothing—patients excited themselves about nothing at all—but whatever it was it was life and death to the man on her front doorstep. This steady-looking man was pitiably distressed, and she wasn't without pity. The nurse knew the symptoms and she knew the drill. It was a very simple one: shock and the counter-shock. . . . She told the truth.

'Miss Francom isn't here.'

Rex Hadley looked back at her. Astonishingly he was almost calm again, but the nurse was in no way astonished. She'd seen it all before, and this one was running to form. Rex asked politely: 'You're sure?'

'I'm not trying to put you off. Why shouldn't I take a message?'

'Do you know where she is?'

'Are you really her fiancé?'

'I've asked her to marry me.'

'She didn't tell us, but I'll tell you this. It's all I know. A hire-car called for her at ten o'clock and we've none of us seen her since.'

Rex took his hat off and the nurse shut the door. Rex climbed into the car again, and thought. He swore for a moment savagely, then switched on the engine.

He started for Cheyne Walk.

The gun came up and the door bell rang imperiously. de Fleury lowered the weapon; he seemed slowly to be recognizing the solid world around him, something he had withdrawn from, lost in another. Mary had seen him like this before, waking from sleep, somewhere between two kingdoms. Then he would yawn and stretch, and finally he'd smile at her; he'd be Francis de Fleury, whole. Now he neither yawned nor stretched, but he rose with a hint of stiffness. He walked to the front door but he left the gun behind him. Mary, with a little gasp, forced herself to pocket it.

When de Fleury came back Rex Hadley was with him. He was looking at Mary Francom, very white. Mary stood motionless, silent and in misery. There was nothing to say. de Fleury was silent too, but he was watching Rex closely. He was puzzled but he was something more. At last he said, deliberately banal: 'I think you know Miss Francom. You met her at Sestriere and again at this flat.'

'We've met many times since then.' Rex Hadley's voice was stony.

'Indeed?'

'I hadn't expected to find her here.'

Mary said shakily: 'Rex. . . .'

He didn't turn towards her. de Fleury was watching still, weighing a decision. Finally he took it. He waved at chairs, sat down himself. He said socially, very cool: 'We'd better have this out.'

'There's nothing to discuss.'

'I'm not quite insensitive. Tell me.'

Rex thought it over, shrugged; in the same dead voice he said: 'I'd asked Miss Francom to marry me.'

'That is the truth? Forgive me, but I must know.'

'It is.'

Astonishingly de Fleury smiled. He began to talk with a calm assurance, a man aware of obligation, decently discharging it. 'Then since I want you to believe me I'll disclose my own interest. I was going to propose myself.'

Rex had looked up but de Fleury didn't wait for him. 'I *intended* to propose; I do not now. Miss Francom has surprised me.'

'We've that in common.'

de Fleury said firmly: 'But you are totally mistaken. So was I. The essential is that Mary is an agent. If that surprises you it shattered me, since I'm another. I imagine she works for the Security Executive, but if she doesn't it will be for something similar. I didn't know that at Sestriere, I didn't in fact discover till tonight. Naturally it was a blow to me. I nearly did something foolish and I must thank your arrival that I didn't. I don't ask why you came here since I'm not now concerned. But you tell me you're engaged— you've a right to the truth. Which is that Mary is *against* me. She has been all along. She was covering me at Sestriere and she's been covering me since. If it interests you I haven't in fact seen her since that evening at this flat. That affair, by the way, has become a little clearer.' de Fleury was speaking pleasantly, quite without resentment. 'Be that as it may, she came here tonight with another specific task. You remember that tape? She came here to steal it. I assume that was on the instructions of her employers but I don't assume too hard. I don't think her motive matters to me now.' For an instant de Fleury's eyes flickered across the table by his chair. 'I could hope you would believe my word, but I can offer a sort of proof. Frisk her and you'll find a gun. Ordinary nurses don't carry them. Nor common mistresses.' He rose, not stiffly now, walking to the door and holding it. 'Good night,' he said. 'Congratulations.'

Rex Hadley was silent, searching de Fleury's face. Presently he said awkwardly: 'You're a very strange man.'

'I am? Mary was saying the same. But I try to be consistent in my strangeness. And don't forget that tape.' He nodded at the bureau. 'You'll find it in there.'

'You mean it?'

'Why not? Apart from what's happened this evening you'll be *au courant* with developments; you'll know it's no use to me, so take it.' de Fleury smiled again. 'Take it as a wedding present.'

They went past him silently, Mary's arm in Rex's. He started the car and drove for perhaps a mile. At length he said: 'I ought to hate that man—I don't. He'd have broken me ruthlessly, but he lives by his own queer rules. You know, I rather like him.'

Mary sighed sleepily, taking his free hand. It was an occasion for a cliché and she wasn't embarrassed by it.

'He's out of this world.'

But Colonel Charles Russell was not. By the end of the next evening he had spent an exceptionally busy day, and it hadn't been wholly an unsatisfactory one. On the debit side eight thugs had died, two of them most unpleasantly, and Russell, a loyal and conscientious master, didn't regard eight foreign mercenaries as an adequate exchange for George Perkins and the crew of the patrol car. Eight animals for four good men—it simply wasn't good enough. But that apart, the affair had its compensations. Not the least to a senior security officer was to observe the politicians squarely stuck with a responsibility which for once they couldn't shuffle back on the Executive. Eight men of a foreign race had died, but one had been left savaged (who might live or might not) and another had reached the wood, firing the rocket which had warned away the helicopters. Both these men had been taken and were now in custody; both were political embarrassments of the very first class, even though almost certainly they wouldn't talk.

It was Russell's guess that there would be no serious attempt to make them. He smiled sardonically. It was fortunate that in de Fleury's country there was no Mister President with a fourteen handicap at golf which he'd never once played to and a misplaced sense of personal responsibility. Nobody was going to strike an attitude, nobody was going to say: 'I authorized this myself.' On the contrary the technique would be one which to Russell was both normal and acceptable. It would be the technique of the Great Big Lie. Charles Russell didn't resent it, for it was part of the established rules; moreover it averted a great deal of trouble—the collapse of important conferences, even the possibility of war. When an agent was captured you automatically disowned him. Only a fool, an amateur, thought otherwise. So the authorities of de Fleury's country would simply deny all knowledge.

And they would probably get away with it.

. . . Anti-tank mines, helicopters, men in a sort of uniform? Russell's smile broadened. Once again they had all been fortunate. It was particularly fortunate that in de Fleury's country there was something approaching two rival governments, and that naturally Her Majesty's could recognize only one of them. Recognize and therefore hold responsible. But 'rival government' wasn't too serious an exaggeration: the other might not be in a position to overthrow the tall man, or at any rate not yet, but there was an organized and well-directed movement. That was the native word—a movement. And since an influential part of the tall man's army was overtly or secretly behind it, it wasn't incredible that military apparatus should somehow have become available. 'Available' was another convenient word since it begged all the awkward questions.

Her Majesty's government would do the same. The Press was already screaming, and when the popular Press was screaming any British government reached for a sedative. Russell was confident it would be offered one. The tall man would send one of his stiff little notes, and it would be a model of cool propriety and of the lie-within-the-rules. The Marshal wouldn't deny the nationality of the men concerned because to do so would be stupid and he was anything but that: instead he'd express profound regret. The perpetrators of this outrage, the men who had dared to plan it, would be pursued remorselessly. He'd even offer compensation to the families of the bereaved, and it would be generous compensation too. Come to think of it there needn't be an actual lie, only the lie by inference. The two prisoners wouldn't talk voluntarily, and later they wouldn't be encouraged to make statements which would be embarrassing internationally. No doubt they'd have their story and they'd be allowed to stick to it. Provided, that is, it didn't involve the tall man or his government. Which it would not. Russell didn't doubt that discreet instructions had already been given to the interrogators. Who weren't his own men, thank God.

So two murderers would be tried for murder and found guilty. The Press would go to town on it, every man in the country would guess the truth, but officially there wouldn't be a whisper. There couldn't be. A formal breach of diplomatic relations would be a disaster to NATO, and moreover the Foreign Office could be relied on to throw its weight against it—its personal weight, since a breach of relations meant the loss of an embassy and of the jobs which went with it. To the career diplomatists that would be final.

Charles Russell chuckled. The diplomats aside, the two countries had a mutual interest in a hush-up, so a hush-up there would be. It was essential politically, though it wouldn't be easy. The Foreign Secretary was in for a very bad week. Russell wasn't without sympathy for the politician who called himself modestly Her Majesty's Principal Secretary of State for Foreign Affairs.

He mixed himself a drink, still laughing quietly. He could afford to laugh. He had done his duty and for once that was enough. They'd push the thing under the carpet, but they couldn't push it back on him. Mostly they tried to but this time they couldn't. Charles Russell was pleased. He had a strong sense of justice and for once this was just.

And descending from high policy to individuals, Francis de Fleury had simply disappeared. That had been predictable. His embassy was extremely busy, the ritual dance was on, but it had found time to mention casually that its military attaché had gone on leave.

Naturally it had been arranged some time ago—that had been mentioned too. Charles Russell had nodded appreciatively: de Fleury's embassy wasn't incompetent. He was privately certain that de Fleury had had no hand in the affair at Maldington, but he could hardly not have known of it. In any case the heat was on. de Fleury wasn't a murderer but he had attempted blackmail, a common crime not normally covered by diplomatic immunity. Victor's outrage at Maldington was going to be quietly smothered, or rather any official connection with it, but if public opinion became sufficiently restive it wouldn't be unnatural to look for a scapegoat elsewhere, in which case de Fleury would be an evident candidate. That was how de Fleury's ambassador would have seen it, and Russell agreed with him. He'd have done the same himself. And there hadn't been stupid slips in detail. The lease on de Fleury's flat was running still, letters were being delivered. . . .

But he'd never return. Sometime, after a month say, there'd be a quiet change in postings. Charles Russell nodded again approvingly. de Fleury's His Excellency was clearly a professional, and Russell, another, respected him.

He finished his drink reflectively; he had private reasons too for a modest satisfaction. He detested unnecessary complications, and the relationship between Rex Hadley and Mary Francom had been dangerously complicated. On the one hand Russell had brought them together; he'd been next door to a matrimonial agency and, since he liked them both, he could reasonably congratulate himself. But on the other he'd been employing Mary to cover Francis de Fleury, and as events had broken that had also meant covering Rex. Russell hadn't liked it. It was true he had told Mary Francom that she could disengage herself, but that was no guarantee that at some time in the future Rex wouldn't discover the real position. After three or four years of marriage, when the first high gloss was wearing thin, a man wouldn't be pleased to hear that his wife had been spying on him.

But now he already knew. And the knowledge had come to him

in the most favourable of lights. Mary had been lucky. . . . Using her position as an agent to steal something which might damage her future husband, not having to excuse herself when he had discovered her in another man's flat but having it all explained, why she lived with de Fleury at all, convincing and corroborated, very much better than anything she could have said herself. . . . Yes, Mary had been fortunate, which meant that Rex had too. de Fleury had behaved admirably.

An unusual character and an unusual day. There was one small end to tuck away, but Mortimer would deal with that. Colonel Russell sent for him.

CHAPTER XII

Robert Mortimer came in tired, grateful for the whisky which Russell at once offered. Russell had had more than one, and he began to talk comfortably. 'I expect you've had a day—I know I have. But there's one small thing still. Victor has had two failures, the first little outrage nipped in the bud by your patrol car and the success of the second prevented by that very brave man George Perkins. And Rex Hadley was the target in both, alone the first time, the second with Doctor Walther. That doesn't mean he will remain so, indeed if I were Victor I should feel it was better to try something else. But then I'm not Victor. We still ought to keep an eye on Hadley.'

Mortimer at once agreed: 'On the face of it Victor would lie low for a bit, but with a man like that you can never be sure. Still, in the ordinary way I'd have been happy enough about Hadley. For one thing he now knows everything. He obviously knows about the second attempt, so I told him about the first. It wouldn't now be embarrassing to attach to him a perfectly open bodyguard, and in the ordinary way I'd do it.'

'Then what's un-ordinary?'

'Did you know he was going abroad tonight?'

Russell sat up sharply. 'You didn't tell me that.'

'I didn't know till half an hour ago, sir. Rex Hadley rang me. It's something to do with Sir William Banner.'

'I like Bill Banner. He's loyal and generous, but he's apt to be quick on the trigger.'

'I gather he's been all three. When Hadley originally took over at Maldington Banner insisted on his taking a holiday. It wasn't convenient to take it all at once, but he went on the first leg to Sestriere. That, as you know, is where de Fleury started working on him. de Fleury doesn't matter now, but there was the rest of that holiday to come, and Banner has decided that this is the moment for it. Decision is the word, I think: Banner insisted again—put it as an order. Not that that was stupid. That affair at Maldington would have been a shock to any man, and going abroad does get Hadley away from the reporters. I don't think we should have objected in principle if Banner had consulted us, but what we might have thought twice about is where Hadley has chosen to go. You won't be surprised that he's taking Miss Francom with him.'

'I'm not surprised. And where are they going?'

'They're going back to Sestriere.'

Charles Russell rose; he strode to the wall and back again, said with his back to Mortimer: 'That's uncomfortably near the frontier.'

'You really think that Victor . . . after two failures . . . in another foreign country. . . ?'

'I said Sestriere was uncomfortably near the frontier. That's a geographical fact, not guesswork about Victor.' Russell was unusually terse. 'What have you done?'

'Made use of a bit of luck, sir. I could send a man after Hadley and I will if you think it necessary, but the bit of luck is that I've a very good friend in the Italian service. He's pretty senior by now and he's based at Turin. Naturally I've been telephoning.'

'And?'

'And they've had trouble with Victor themselves. Not on the scale of Maldington, but trouble. They love him no better than we do, and they'll co-operate with gusto. Maraldi himself has already left for Sestriere.'

'You think I should ring his chief?'

'Maraldi's already done so—I told you he was senior. The whole story will be in Rome by now, and all the implications. If indeed there are any. If we're not simply fussing.'

'I don't think we're fussing.' Russell considered. 'You trust this Maraldi?'

Robert Mortimer said carefully: 'I've good reason to think well of him—personal reason. And sending men into foreign countries means butting in on a colleague's territory. That's always delicate.'

'It is indeed.' Russell sat down again. 'You know,' he said reflectively, 'ten minutes ago I was feeling rather good. You could call it self-satisfied if you wanted to be unkind. A good many difficulties, some official, some rather less so, had cleared themselves up or seemed to have. And now there's a doubt again, something to nag me.' He picked up his glass, turning it in his hand, staring at what was left in it. 'To Rex Hadley and Mary. To your friend Maraldi. To our continuing good fortune.'

'To all of them.'

The room that morning had been very hot, even for a nation which detested to be cold. The furniture was public property, grand and very ugly. The heat had long since spoiled the marqueterie.

In it Victor was having a very bad quarter of an hour with the tall man. He had expected a bad quarter of an hour, a reprimand at least, and that he would have accepted since he was a soldier and disciplined. But he had hoped that the Marshal would for once be explicit: instead he was in really dreadful form, saying almost anything but what Victor needed to hear. The direct question he deliberately ducked. It was a very simple one: was Victor or was he not still in charge of the Bureau which he had previously commanded? Was he, to put it bluntly, sacked?

But the tall man had talked on. Country, he said, and honour. The motherland. Glory. Victor had heard it before, and it had ceased even to amuse him. He was a brave and dedicated man but with the mistrust of words of the decent bourgeois. The tall man hadn't made it easier for him by not allowing himself even a hint of recrimination, and Victor knew that if their positions had been reversed he would himself have been both rude and angry. He resented that the tall man's technique was precisely calculated to put him at a disadvantage. Somehow they could always do that—the tall men and the de Fleurys; somehow they could always wrong-foot you. Where he himself would have ranted and raved the tall man was polite and even generous. And they made you listen absurdly carefully. It wasn't what they said but what they didn't.

Victor had been listening absurdly carefully, and it had tired him. He was an irascible man, and anger he could have understood. If the Marshal had struck him. . . .

He hadn't been within a mile of it; he hadn't mentioned failure, only the steps which failure had now made necessary. The tall man, it seemed, was confident that he could take them. His country had something which the English wanted badly: without his cooperation they wouldn't obtain it easily and, if he really opposed the plan, probably not at all. So they wouldn't press the Maldington affair too rigorously. There was an ugly crack in the diplomatic wall but a strong mutual interest in papering it over. The tame cat diplomatists were kept for exactly that.

The tall man's manner had slightly but significantly changed. . . . Not that the appearances of diplomatic relations had anything to do with the realities of international politics. The tall man still wanted Project A. What, then, was Victor now proposing?

Victor had begun to talk in turn, but the tall man had maddeningly lost interest. With a flick of his hands he had stopped Victor dead. Victor had felt himself flush and the Marshal had smiled aloofly. They had been at military school together, but that hadn't bridged their difference. Then what, Victor had asked finally, were the Marshal's instructions?

. . . Ah, instructions. But the tall man had no qualifications to give instructions in a matter which he didn't understand in detail.

(And by inescapable inference did not wish to.) He had stated his requirement, which was knowledge of Project A. The details were for the experts, and Victor was chief of experts.

Victor had drawn a deliberate breath. Then might he take it that he still had authority. . . ?

. . . Ah, authority. It was a difficult word in a difficult situation. It rather depended. The experts, what you might call the *working* experts, had made rather a fiasco, hadn't they? Perhaps a closer interest, a more *personal* approach. . . . For the first time the tall man had permitted himself a direct statement. Looking steadily at Victor he had said: 'You're not an old man yet.'

He had risen and shaken hands formally; then he had stalked from the room.

Victor took a taxi to his spartan flat. He lived alone, and he began to cook his midday meal. He cooked simply but well, deft and experienced. There was soup in a huge stock pot and he began to heat it. The *bonne à tout faire* was having her day off, but she had left him bread and salad. His steak he had bought himself. He put it under the grill, mixing his salad, pouring a glass of wine. He hadn't a doubt what the tall man had meant. He, Victor Toit, of modest birth but with a lifetime of selfless service to the state, had been offered a final chance. Or rather it had been tossed at him. A final, a personal chance.

He stirred the soup reflectively, then, holding his wine, he walked to a mirror. . . . Sixty-four years and all of them had been hard ones. And so was he hard himself. He was putting on weight but he wasn't flabby. He smiled at his empty sleeve: the other arm was good still. . . . Sixty-four years and a job which was his life. With any luck he'd die in it for there was nothing outside. Women had been concessions to a young man's need: he'd never dared marry. He had a daughter and sometimes he sent her money, but they hadn't met for years. No, there was nothing outside.

Victor sat down to eat. . . . A final, a private chance. And Hadley and some woman intended to return to Sestriere. That snippet of information had just come in. Victor's smile had been experienced and a little sad. Where there was a woman there were always possibilities.

Russell and Robert Mortimer drank to their continuing good luck, and both put their glasses down. One of four telephones on Russell's desk rang stridently and Russell picked it up. He listened for a moment, frowning and puzzled, then he handed it to Mortimer. 'Someone's talking in Italian. He's asking for you.'

Robert Mortimer listened in turn. '*D'accordo*,' he said finally, hanging up. He looked at Russell, intent and serious. 'That was Maraldi. Victor has just arrived in Sestriere.'

Mortimer had affection for Charles Russell and a real respect, and at the moment the respect was uppermost. Russell wasn't exactly young and his day had been exhausting. But now he rose steadily, pouring more whisky. He returned with the two glasses, sitting at his desk again; he said almost casually: 'And to think that five minutes ago I was talking about a certain doubt returning, a tiny sore to nag me.' His manner changed abruptly. 'You're sure, of course?'

'Maraldi's sure—he's seen Victor himself. Victor isn't disguised or anything melodramatic. He's staying there quite openly, using his own name. But he's arrived in Sestriere. He must have flown south, then motored up. In any case he's there.'

'And what does Maraldi suggest?'

'He's too experienced to panic. He's on his own ground and he's recognized Victor. He'll double-up on anything done already; he'll take every precaution possible.'

Russell thought it over. 'And we ourselves? It's not our bailiwick, we're not formally responsible—the safe game is simply to stay out of it.' He smiled an Executive smile. 'But I like Rex Hadley and I'm fond of Mary Francom. And I'm not a civil servant.'

Robert said slowly: 'We were talking about sending a man of our own.'

'All right, we'll talk again. You'll have to work fast, though.'
'I shall.'
'Can you get him away tonight?'
Major Mortimer stood up. 'I only need to pack,' he said.

Robert caught a plane to Milan in the small hours. It was by no means the quickest route, but he knew that Rex and Mary were flying to Turin and he didn't want to risk them seeing him—their surprise and the need to explain himself. He arrived at Milan in the dark still, thinking himself lucky to find a taxi. There was a brief but explosive haggle, the inevitable and amiable agreement. They drove across the Lombard plain, the Fiat's headlamps scything the almost deserted autostrada. Robert nodded dully for he was tired and dirty and he hated both. As they began to climb the cold woke him brutally. It was dark still as they stopped, and Robert paid off the taxi. He had refused a hotel but had accepted the name of a modest *pensione*. The car couldn't reach it but he had instructions how to get there. He walked away with his bag, the *tassista* staring, shrugging. . . . A well-to-do gentleman and he was going to Aunt Anna's. The English were verily mad.

The house had begun to stir, for these were mountain people, early risers. Robert Mortimer booked a room. Bed wasn't worth considering, but he bathed and shaved; he opened the double window and the alpine air revived him; he rang for his coffee and drank it with pleasure.

Half an hour later he went down to the simple dining-room. The first man he saw was Francis de Fleury. de Fleury bowed politely, wishing him good morning in Italian. . . . The signore was here for long? He would find the snow excellent. There hadn't been a flicker of recognition. de Fleury didn't know him—didn't want to.

CHAPTER XIII

Robert Mortimer was a tactful man, too tactful to rush Maraldi. He knew that his arrival wouldn't have passed unnoticed—in the circumstances nobody's arrival would pass unnoticed—and he gave Maraldi twenty-four hours to get in touch with him. When he did not Robert felt free to take the initiative, and on his second day he walked down to the ski school after breakfast. The classes were being sorted into groups by patient instructors, and a man was leaning against the wooden barrier. Like Robert he wasn't in ski-ing clothes. He nodded cheerfully as Robert came up. 'It's nice to see you, and we needn't pretend not to know each other. Naturally I've been busy or I'd have called on you before. I'm staying at the Conte under my own name, and Mr. Hadley and Miss Francom are there too. Victor is at the Vallata, also under his proper name.' Maraldi laughed. 'This seems to be routine, but just the same I'm delighted to see you. Come and talk it over.'

They strolled away across the snow and Maraldi asked: 'Do you intend to ski?'

'I can't. As it happens I've never been in a winter sports resort before. This is an eye-opener.' Robert stopped, looking about him at the wide nursery slopes. It was early still but the ski-lifts were busy. Groups passed on the way to them, some chattering, some serious, polyglot and colourful. The sun was warming from a cloudless sky, the air was superb. Robert filled his lungs. 'Maybe I've been missing something.'

Maraldi shrugged. 'It's a habit like another. If you start young enough it gets you hopelessly. Your life revolves round a winter fortnight in the snow.'

'It's more crowded than I expected.'

'There are a great many French. The snow across the frontier is pretty poor, so they've flocked up here. And today is a public holiday. People start from Torino at dawn and motor up. They're the genuine enthusiasts, but they bring nothing to the posh hotels and the managements don't like them.' Maraldi's voice changed. 'However, we've no great interest in anybody coming in for a day's skiing and leaving again at night. We're concerned with certain residents.'

'Starting with Victor.'

'Quite. And I can't see what he's doing here; I can't see what he *thinks* he's doing. . . . Another attempt at kidnapping Hadley? But humanly speaking that's out. For one thing I don't think his own people would allow him to try that again. I've been reading the English papers and they're pretty explosive. So is the international situation and I just don't believe that Victor's masters would let him blow it finally. That's an opinion of theory, but on the practical side this isn't at all a good place for a kidnapping, especially if your opponents are on notice of the possibility. Admittedly the frontier's pretty close, but at this time of year and with this sort of snow there's no slipping a body across it by some mountain path. There are just two ways across by road, and you can take it that both posts have been alerted.' Maraldi waved a Latin hand. 'You may trust me,' he said.

'Of course.'

'Then come and have a drink.'

They walked to the ski club, ordering coffee and Vecchia Romagna. Robert tackled them with appetite. He was feeling extraordinarily well—so well he was obliged to remind himself that he mustn't be over-optimistic. He liked Maraldi for he had very good reason to, but when it came to detail. . . .

135

Perhaps it was just his manner.

Robert drank reflectively. He had told Charles Russell that Maraldi was a colleague of long standing, and in fact he was something more. It had begun by Robert capturing him in the Western Desert. It had been an honourable capture too. Maraldi's Division had been the Ariete, and it had fought extremely well. He had been far from the incredible rabble clamouring for the bag, its sheer weight almost breaking the administrative machine, almost turning what had been victory into a defeat. Maraldi had been taken honourably, and he had honourably escaped at the first opportunity. In the circumstances it hadn't been difficult. And several years later, in Italy itself, Robert too had been captured, escaping in turn and much more arduously. He had been picked up starving by a band of *partigiani*, and Maraldi had been its leader. Robert had stayed with them for seven months. They hadn't, he knew, been wasted.

They hadn't been wasted but they had been very irregular, and Robert Mortimer, painstakingly trained in the Security Executive, had since learnt to mistrust the irregular. Angelo Maraldi, for example. He was competent and resourceful—Robert had seen him working—but he wouldn't have inspired confidence in the top corridors of Whitehall. For one thing he laughed too easily, and that was always fatal.

Robert was in a difficulty: this wasn't his manor but Angelo's; he couldn't interfere and he mustn't appear to be probing. He ordered more brandy, saying across it casually: 'So Victor's at the Vallata and it won't be another snatch. Then what is he up to?'

There was a formidable shrug again. 'Your guess is as good as mine.'

'Oh no. I'm English, and we're bad at guessing.'

'And I've acquired some of your dislike of it. So far it's a little like one of those tediously contemporary crime stories—I mean that there's nothing to go on, no respectable normal motive, so you buy a handbook of psychiatry and push it along from there. Victor has had a considerable failure, and I don't think his masters would let

136

him forget it. What's more he's getting on. No man of that age and with a career like that behind him would want to leave in failure. Men of that age act strangely.'

'Then he's been acting oddly?'

'Yes, in a sense, since so far he's done nothing. I needn't say he's covered every second of the day. So for that matter are Hadley and Miss Francom, but he's made no attempt to meet them, far less to act. Yesterday he went for a little walk, watching the skiers, and in the evening he drank in a bar; he might be a widower in advanced middle age enjoying his first holiday alone for years. And he seems to have a passion for the cableways, all three of them, but that isn't unusual when you neither ski nor skate. He had lunch in the restaurant at the top of Banchetta, chatting to the engineers. It's all very innocent, quite beyond a policeman, so out with the mumbo-jumbo book.'

'I'd rather stay a policeman.' Robert considered. 'But what does he *have* here—people, I mean?'

Maraldi's brown face crinkled shrewdly. 'I know what you're thinking . . . Maraldi—not a bad chap, efficient enough in a slapdash way, but Italian of course, and over details——'

'I was thinking no such thing.'

'*Caro mio*, be quiet! You are English and I can read you like a book. I always could. In any case the question was perfectly reasonable, so I'll give you the answer. We've checked every soul with a bed in this village, and we know enough about Victor's people to feel confident that if one of them tried to come up here we could spot him. That has meant committing a good many men, but you can take it I've committed them. In any case, to do anything effective Victor would need more than a single man. That would mean a gang of them, with proportionately better chances of noticing anybody odd. No, all Victor has here is a couple of honest stooges. Pretty lowly ones at that. The second porter at the Vallata is one of his men, but he's every bit as old as Victor. He'll bring or send messages, he's Victor's ears, but he's never been a strongarm. And there's a man in the transformer house who once did a job for him. That was ten years ago and he wasn't Italian then. He's not a rough either.'

'Has Victor been meeting them?'

'So far as the porter goes, of course. But they're both too experienced to have given anything away. And as for the electrician, Victor hailed him in a bar quite openly last night. He hailed him as a friend in arms from days in Indo-China, and it happens to be true. They had three drinks and that was that.'

'And Francis de Fleury?'

Robert had expected a mild surprise but Maraldi disappointed him. 'I know you're staying at Aunt Anna's too. It's the best food in town if you like native cooking.'

'de Fleury seems to.'

Maraldi said firmly: 'I'm not worried about de Fleury. He's an ex-military attaché and he'll be carrying the can. They wouldn't dare use him, not in any way at all. He'd be spotted at once, as indeed he has been.'

'Then why is he here?'

'He's a professional blackmailer and this is a fashionable resort. There are a good many men here, rich, and mostly they're married. There are also pretty women and alone. What better stalking ground?'

'I can't dispute the theory.' Mortimer sounded doubtful, but Maraldi said equably: 'But it isn't only theory. If you'll allow me to say so we've again done our homework. de Fleury was here at Christmas and he was booked to return.'

'We knew that too. If Rex Hadley had come back here then de Fleury could have followed him.'

'So he *has* come back. No doubt with a different object but at least there's nothing strange about his presence. He had somewhere to go to when his work for Victor crashed, and a standing professional motive. He was booked at the Conte and he's changed to Aunt Anna's, but I hardly think that's sinister. The Conte costs money and he's just lost a job. But he can drink at the Conte's bars, dance there if he wants to, *operate*——'

'Has he spoken to Rex Hadley?'

'No.'

'To Mary Francom?'

'They met face to face in the Conte. He bowed and she smiled at him. I'm told it was a friendly smile.'

'de Fleury deserved it.' Robert Mortimer thought again; the question he was considering could easily seem an impertinence; he said at last tentatively: 'Victor . . . if you could get him out of Sestriere. . . .'

Maraldi sighed patiently but he wasn't offended. 'My very dear friend, I am doing just that. But it isn't so easy. I don't deny that if we had known he was coming we should probably have found something at the frontier, some irregularity in his papers, to turn him back, but once he's in it's quite another matter to eject him. There was a time in this country when a police officer could conduct a foreigner to the frontier for no better reason than that he didn't like his face. Not now. You could call it part of the price of a democracy. Be that as it may, there are now formalities. Rest assured they are in train. In three or four days. . . .' Maraldi spread his hands.

'You almost persuade me——'

But Maraldi had risen; with the first hint of reserve he said: 'But I'm not trying to persuade you except to enjoy yourself. It's a pity you don't ski, but the skating instructress is a charmer.' The reserve disappeared as quickly as it had come. 'A really *beautiful* figure.' Maraldi made a gesture with finger and thumb. 'Quite feasible in a lesson. Delicious. And excellent exercise—skating, I mean.' He held out a friendly hand. 'I don't think I ought to ask you to the Conte when Hadley and Miss Francom are there too, but I'll drop in at Aunt Anna's. If you happen to want me urgently I'm mostly around the rink. But I don't think you will.'

He strolled away.

Robert Mortimer walked back to lunch. Maraldi had been

reassuring—logical. Robert sighed softly. It was Charles Russell's favourite precept that in security logic meant nothing.

Rex Hadley woke in the night at the Conte. He lay silently, watching Mary. She slept on her back but she didn't snore. Irene had snored intolerably. Remorselessly articulate awake she hadn't in sleep been merciful. But Mary breathed evenly beside him. He loved her, he thought, but he didn't yet know her. So much the more exciting for the future. He didn't understand her. For instance in the matter of de Fleury. Naturally they had discussed that extraordinary evening at his flat. . . . Waving a gun at a woman he claimed to love, threatening to kill her and apparently meaning to, and all because he had discovered she was an agent. Who had been spying on him certainly, who had done her job well. But pointing a pistol, talking incomprehensibly about betrayals. . . . To Rex it had been simply an outrage—the man had been drunk or touched. He had said so to Mary and she'd quietly agreed. Perhaps, he thought now, too quietly. She too has been thinking, and her conclusions weren't as simple as his own. She hadn't explained and maybe she couldn't. Rex Hadley smiled. He wasn't jealous of de Fleury for he had very good reason not to be.

He slipped from the warm bed carefully, walking to the window, pulling the curtain and catching his breath. The moon rode serenely, crowning Banchetta, flooding the white valley in inhuman light, etching the firs the starkest black. The snow had a private life, something apart from men. The pylons of the cableway strode up the mountain purposefully, man's only intrusion in a world which wasn't his.

An intrusion but a convenience: the run from the top of Banchetta was one of the pleasantest. With a little more practice Rex felt he could manage it, and Mary had always ski-ed well. The piste would be fun in the evening, marvellous as the moon rose. He must look at the calendar, work out the timings. The cableway closed down at dusk, but it shouldn't be impossible to make arrangements. A few thousand lire should do it.

Rex went back to bed, his hands behind his head. He didn't expect to sleep again. The busiest days of his life were only just behind him, and he had been grateful for the activity since he hadn't had time to think. There had been statements to the discreetest of officials, other officials, discreet again but unmistakably firm, to help him with the pressing attentions of the newspapers; then a visit from Sir William Banner and the unequivocal instruction to take himself off on holiday. All this he had welcomed, for he had known subconsciously that a revulsion was inevitable. He had soon thrown off the physical shock of being shot over in his forties, but he knew that he wasn't scathless. Sooner or later his mind would pay what healthy nerves refused to.

Suddenly he was terrified. He'd never quite believed it all—something had happened but not to himself. Major Mortimer had told him about an earlier attempt, and probably he'd looked incredulous, for Mortimer had explained with deadly under-emphasis. There had been a research worker in Dortmund who had been beaten to death for the secret of some automatic mortar, and Project A was a great deal more important than a mortar. Rex had at once understood, but instinctively he had rejected the implications. Dortmund was in a foreign land, and this extraordinary organization Mortimer had talked about, somebody called Victor, utterly ruthless—all these were foreign too. It couldn't happen here.

And now it had and more than once. The second attempt they'd almost got him. Project A wasn't yet a secret in the normal sense, but Rex knew its progress. So suppose they had taken him. He stiffened suddenly. There was something called interrogation, and nowadays it didn't mean asking questions. Major Mortimer had been serious about Victor: Victor would stick at nothing. Rex had seen too much pain to believe that men could resist it long. From the Inquisition to the cellars of the Gestapo, sooner or later the bravest talked, and he wasn't especially brave, or didn't think so. The stiffening broke in a shaken shudder. So what would he have told them?

That if Project A succeeded there would be a conventional explosive ten or twenty times as powerful as anything previously known. Which could be fatal to a fading Power whose only real asset in the international free-for-all was the mass of its conscript army. But that they would know already. So a little more fire and a little more iron and, and. . . .

That if you took certain chemicals, none of them esoteric, but put them with a catalyst which a chemist had stumbled on by accident; that if you froze them down to absolute zero or nearly, tenths of a degree, then hundredths, then finally perhaps. . . .

That would be the truth but they might not accept it. Not at once certainly, perhaps not at all. So days of it, weeks, screaming your ignorance at emotionless professional faces, finally a cripple, impotent. . . .

Rex slipped out of bed again, caught in a horror he had known was inevitable but had somehow contrived to stifle. He ran a bath quietly for he had begun to sweat; he lay in the lukewarm water motionless, trying to relax. He climbed from the bath at last, towelling himself slowly, careful not to sweat again.

When he returned to the bedroom the bedside light was on. Mary was sitting up and watching him. As she saw his face her own changed quickly.

'Rex, what's the matter?'

He hesitated; told her shamefacedly.

'Come here.'

He went across to her, uncertain still. When he was near she said: 'But I know about that—dear God, I know.'

'You never told me they tortured you.'

'They never caught me. It wasn't the thing but the fear of it, the nightmare always with you. Oh yes, I know all right.'

'I suppose I'm a bit of a coward.'

Astonishingly she began to laugh.

'Is that so funny?' He spoke without anger.

'Of course.' Through the laughter she said unevenly: 'Dear Rex, you're very English. I love you but you're a stranger. The English don't think about courage. Sometimes they think about fear, and then they sweat.'

'Yes, I've been sweating.'

'A waste of time.' She slid down into the bed again, said suddenly, unexpectedly: 'I'd hate to be up against you.'

'You said that once before to me.'

'It's all you need to know.' She took his arms and pulled him down, holding him firmly.

Not for the first time Rex Hadley drew strength from her.

Victor's thinking had been as logical as Maraldi's and his conclusions more precise. He had come to Sestriere without a definite plan, almost on impulse if he had been capable of such a thing. He knew he was on probation, but he hadn't supposed that the tall man would be so stupid as to put him on trial but remove from him all authority and the tools of his trade. Nor had he. Maraldi had been right that Victor had only two agents in Sestriere and that neither was a thug, but he had something else which Maraldi hadn't spotted. It was a record-player of a popular make, and unless you had been sufficiently interested to take it to pieces that was what it passed for. Victor started it at six o'clock every evening. His taste in music was the severest—the Lydian quartets and Gregorian chants as formalized as a bull fight. Then at half-past six precisely he stacked his records, pressing a hidden switch. The pre-tuned curcuit wasn't especially powerful but it was efficient over thirty miles, and thirty miles away across the frontier were Victor's real ears.

As it happened they had sent to him only once, but the message had made him think furiously. Mr. J. Wallis Danziger was leaving Washington for England, and most men had heard of J. Wallis Danziger.

Victor had heard plenty. Danziger had been smuggled out of Germany in 1945 under the noses of the Russians and taken to America. There his career had been remarkable, since he had not only kept himself in the first flight of physicists but had amassed a fortune applying his knowledge. Victor smiled ironically. That wouldn't have been possible in Europe: the European tradition was that a top-grade scientist shouldn't also be successful as an industrialist. Even to try seemed somehow a little wicked. The facts remained that in America Danziger had established himself as a considerable tycoon, and that Danziger was flying to England. The Marshal would know that too. He wouldn't like it. . . . Those intolerable Anglo-Saxons were getting together again. To exclude him, of course, and finally. And Danziger hadn't booked in London but was going direct to Birmingham. Where no doubt he would talk with Sir William Banner. Victor was sure of it. The Danzigers of the world didn't fly round it for pleasure. The English *did* have something and the Americans wished to share.

Victor frowned intently. He had less time than ever now. Danziger's journey meant that Project A had succeeded, or at least that there had been an essential advance, and of those who would know the secret Rex Hadley still stood first. Victor nodded briefly. . . . And so? He had already dismissed another attempt at kidnapping. He himself would not have shrunk from it, but he didn't believe it would be permitted. The tall man hadn't stripped him of authority, he could still receive news, give reasonable orders to subordinates who would obey him, but to organize another snatch would mean orders of a kind which the Marshal must inevitably hear of. Whereupon he would countermand them. So Victor was back on routine resources, and in Sestriere they weren't impressive. But in theory the problem was unchanged: essentially it was still to get Hadley alone for half an hour or better. . . . No, it *had* changed. Hadley had a woman with him, one he intended to marry. So get them together, both of them. Go to work on the woman and the man would talk in no time.

The Church had exploited that one, the Dominican Inquisitors. Victor smiled grimly. Where there was a woman there were indeed possibilities.

He put on another record, not listening but thinking. So all he need do was get Hadley and this girl of his alone for half an hour. But that looked impossible—he hadn't a hope. He knew that he was watched. It was being done competently, but he was too experienced to miss it. He had recognized Maraldi, which meant that the whole machine was on notice and in gear against him. And the porter had told him of de Fleury's arrival. Who was probably now working for the other side. The rat. Not that a playboy mattered.

It had once occurred to Victor that in Sestriere there was just one place where it might be possible to be alone with Hadley. It was about the size of an ordinary lift and it could be made entirely private. But he couldn't see how to do it. The shot wasn't on.

He put on his coat and went for a walk, spotting his shadower but ignoring him. The lights of the township were coming on, climbing up the hillside from chalets and *pensioni*, shining invitingly from the shops in the Portico. Victor walked into the colonnade. From the tea-room a dance band thumped indifferently, and a man was singing in a vacuous tenor. Victor loathed popular tenors. Italian tenors sang with their testicles and the Irish indulged a wholly repellent edge. He would have admitted that he was in a very bad temper. The careless gaiety offended him. He stood with his legs apart, head forward, unconsciously scowling; he scowled at the knots of girls, enticingly entrousered; he scowled at the lean brown boys. Many were his compatriots. . . . Degenerates, accepting too casually an ease they hadn't earned, children of a class which was destroying the old values. What did they know of the world they encumbered, of decent discipline, of hot doomed forts in some tropical ricefield? Of impotent internationalists negotiating not for the lives of the garrison but for the face of two potentates not even directly engaged? Victor looked down at his empty sleeve and his mouth twisted angrily.

He began to walk towards the ski club—at least he would be spared the band there. It was warm in the hall and he walked to the bar. The instructors were stacking their skis, rubbing their legs and chatting. In its neat little bay the cable-car to Alpette was already parked, but the last from Banchetta was just coming in. Victor took his brandy to the window, watching it as it slid safely home.

. . . No bigger than a lift. Three people could be quite alone there.

Presently the attendant came in. He stamped his cold feet and walked to the bar. There Victor joined him for he knew him already. He had spent a good deal of time on the cableways—Maraldi had noticed it. Victor bought more brandy. He had drunk one already and the spirit had restored his self-control, though not his good humour since he owned none. Over the drinks he asked: 'A tiring day?'

The attendant shrugged. 'No worse than usual. But thank God we shut down at dusk.'

'You always do that?'

'Oh yes.' The shrug again. 'Sometimes we're asked to make a special trip—honeymoon couples and when there's a moon.'

Victor's face didn't move and his voice didn't change. 'And does that happen often?'

'They ask, but we don't often do it. It's expensive, you see—we have to make them pay. There was a couple inquiring this evening as it happens. An Englishman. Mad, but the wife was beautiful. Coming down by moonlight. . . . Well, when you're rich. . . .'

'I'd like to do that too.'

'That would be up to him. I heard they were at the Conte.'

'When are they going up?'

'Not for three days. The man had it all worked out. There's a moon on Friday by a quarter to eight, so I'll start them at seven-fifteen.'

'You'll be going up with them?'

'I'm supposed to, but in the circumstances. . . .' There was a tolerant smile. 'They'll come down on skis of course, and we can always

146

pull an empty car down—empty, that is, if you're not yourself in it. It's a very private trip though, and I can't just include you. It's up to you to fix it.'

'At the Conte, I think you said?'

'That's right. An Englishman.'

They exchanged good nights and Victor rose quickly. He walked not to the Conte but direct to the Vallata. For the first time that evening he smiled. Victor knew a break when he saw one.

CHAPTER XIV

Robert Mortimer had enjoyed his supper and had almost finished it. He had been thinking about Maraldi but not too hard, since to think about Maraldi wasn't fruitful. Undeniably he had done everything which Robert would have done himself, and undeniably this was his own territory, not Robert's. It was unfair to be influenced by a certain Latin airiness, unjustified to worry that perhaps. . . .

Robert saw that a man was unexpectedly standing by his table. The man bowed politely, said with some formality, allowing himself the possibility of a retreat: 'My name is de Fleury and we met at London airport. I should like to recall myself.'

It was a maxim in the Executive that over-subtlety was stupid. Robert accepted it gladly, for he didn't feel happy in verbal sparring, with foreigners especially. He left that to Russell. Now he said truthfully: 'I didn't think you wanted to be recognized. Won't you sit down?'

de Fleury did so, glancing round the dining-room. By now it was almost empty. In a voice neither loud nor soft he said: 'We've an interest in common or I wouldn't be intruding.'

'Yes?'

'It's a man called Victor, and I didn't know he was here.' de Fleury was observant and he saw Robert's face change. 'I've no right you should trust me but I hope that you will. A little, that is. I shan't make sense otherwise.'

'Let's begin on the hypothesis that you didn't know Victor was here.' Robert Mortimer was a cautious man.

'Thank you. So I'll tell you something else, though I dare say you know it already. I no longer work for Victor. I owe him no loyalty —if anything, to the contrary.'

'We did guess that.'

'So I'm a blackmailer out of a job, and Sestriere is a natural for a blackmailer. I had a little money saved, enough to stake me, and if I didn't touch here I was moving to San Remo in the spring. And I was *booked* to come back here—that could be verified.'

'It has.'

de Fleury smiled. 'You're thorough,' he said.

'We do what's obvious. Often it's all we can.'

'Then I'd like you to believe one thing, though I'm afraid it isn't obvious at all. I'm not a murderer. I went to London as Victor's agent, and I went because I had to. I was to obtain information from Rex Hadley by means which you now know about. I failed. It wasn't a creditable plan but it had nothing to do with kidnapping, nor the cold-blooded murder of innocent men.' de Fleury straightened suddenly. 'I'd like you to believe me.'

'I don't say I disbelieve you.'

'Then tell me why Victor is here.'

Robert said mildly: 'You're asking me?'

'I am.'

'I only know Hadley's here too.'

'And so is Miss Francom. Hadley's a man I once tried to blackmail. I've never been emotionally involved with him. But Miss Francom. . . .' de Fleury hesitated, seemed to change his mind. 'Mary,' he said, and stopped.

There was a considerable silence whilst both men thought. Robert was thinking that the Victors were the bread and butter of a security officer's life—his own, Maraldi's, that of a hundred others. But the de Fleurys were something different. Robert had gifts, but he knew that imagination wasn't one of them. Normally its absence didn't worry him, but now he felt a need of it. He looked at de Fleury, trying to read him, failing.

de Fleury was a criminal—it was better to stick to that.

But he was speaking again, saying rather stiffly: 'I was attached to Miss Francom and that is an obligation. If Victor should harm either of them. . . .' He rose unexpectedly, clearly on edge. 'I'm a man without honour but I'm not a dishonoured man.'

He walked away.

Robert finished his fruit. The remark had struck him as in very bad taste, the sort of thing only a foreigner would say. Maybe. And he wasn't a foreigner but a conscientious British security officer aware of his limitations. The paradox had been meaningless but it would be stupid to assume that it hadn't been important to de Fleury.

Robert Mortimer sighed. He was out of his depth with scoundrels with a sense of obligation.

He was woken next morning by Aunt Anna's single maid. She brought with her a smile, an undrinkable cup of tea made as a concession to an incomprehensible addiction, and the news that a Signor Maraldi was awaiting him downstairs.

'Please ask him up.'

Mortimer had discreetly disposed of the tea in the washbasin and was shaving as Maraldi came in. Maraldi was in splendid form. He said at once: 'I have very good news—but excellent. Victor has left us.'

Robert considered it. 'And when did he go?'

'Late last night. As it happened he was one jump ahead of us. A message came through from Rome for me, and we were going to pick him up a little later when we could have done it with the minimum people noticing.'

'You think there was a leak?'

'It's possible.' Maraldi shrugged. 'I told you the second porter at the Vallata was one of Victor's men, and the porter has a brother in the telephone exchange. I've been wondering about that brother and now I'll go after him. Not that it matters at the moment. If the wretched man leaked, then in this case he obliged us.' Maraldi was clearly pleased; he didn't rub his hands since that wasn't a Latin gesture, but it was Robert's impression that he would have done so if he had been English. He went on buoyantly: 'So that, I suggest, is that. But I hope you won't leave us just yet. This is a very pleasant place when you're not on some tiresome job.' Maraldi grinned. 'A proposito, how's the skating?'

'I found I could still stand up.'

'Good. Then have lunch with me at the Vallata. A modest celebration.'

'It's a date.'

Maraldi waved gaily and left, and Robert finished dressing. He went downstairs and booked a call to London. It would be an open line, but he didn't have access to another except through Maraldi, and it was Maraldi he wanted to discuss with Russell. In any case, he told himself, smiling a little wryly, any telephone seemed to be suspect. He found that the delay would be less than he had expected and sat down to wait quietly.

Twenty minutes later Charles Russell was saying: 'Yes?'

'It's an open line, sir, but I'll have to risk it.'

'Right.'

'A certain party has left here.'

'Excellent news. And now?'

'It's the now I'm not too happy about. My good friend here is competent, but he's apt to swing high, swing low.'

'You mean he'll relax? Too much, perhaps. He'll let everything go by the board?'

Robert said deliberately: 'There are a good many men involved and no doubt they'll have other commitments. And the powers-that-be aren't generous. Spend a lira too much and you get dropped on.'

'I take your point.'

There was a silence, and Robert had to ask: 'Are you still there, sir?'

'I am. We'll have to chance this line a bit. Now tell me this. A principal has left the stage. What did he leave behind him as supporting cast?'

'Nothing of consequence, and nothing rough. He had an ear in the hotel where he was staying, and there's some sort of electrician, though he hasn't been active for years.'

'You accept that as correct?'

'Unhesitatingly. At that sort of thing my friend's first class.'

'Could anyone new get into the act?'

'He could if they took the doormen off.'

'Which you fear they may do?'

'Well. . . .'

There was another long silence before Russell spoke again. 'And the happy couple we've also an interest in? They know nothing of this, I take it? They're with you still?'

'They are.'

Russell said promptly: 'Then stay till they leave.'

He was gone.

Robert hung up; he wanted to think, to get it on paper as Russell had taught him. He never did. de Fleury was walking up to him, taut as a wire. Without preliminary courtesies he said: 'Victor has left Sestriere.'

'I know. How did you?' Robert, surprised, was a little short.

'It wasn't difficult to find out. We spoke of this before, and I told you I was worried. Frankly, I've been taking an interest in him.' de Fleury smiled. 'In an amateur sort of way, of course. You're a professional.'

'You must know I'm not the only one.'

'I guessed it, and that's what troubles me. If we're talking about your colleagues here. . . . Victor has gone and it all looks good.' de Fleury hesitated, finally said slowly: 'It might look *too* good. Too neat—too final.'

Robert thought it over for he had a difficult decision. He could smile politely and walk away, but a hunch constrained him. He was impressed that de Fleury's instinct wasn't different from his own: there were possibilities of an alliance with a man who feared as he did, and an alliance wasn't something to be lightly repulsed. On the other hand he couldn't see what alliance. de Fleury was a black-mailer, by all accounts a good one, but against the possibility that Victor might not have thrown his hand in the peculiar skills of an extortioner weren't obviously useful. Now if de Fleury had been a tough. . . . Robert could have used an experienced tough.

All too evidently he was not. Robert said in compromise: 'I expect you saw me telephoning, and I was talking to my boss. He told me to stay here till Hadley and Miss Francom left.'

'I'm delighted to hear it. Delighted.'

'Not that I really think. . . . For what I'm worth you could call it an insurance.'

'We'll call you an insurance then. And I'm staying myself and you can call that what you like. I have motive as I hinted, but I doubt if you'll find a word for it.' de Fleury smiled again and turned.

Robert shrugged irritably. He was an experienced security officer with years of precedent to guide him. But Francis de Fleury hadn't a precedent. Experience suggested that Maraldi might relax too much, and Russell, even more experienced, had just thought the same. But Francis de Fleury. . . .

Robert decided that he could use a drink: dealing with de Fleury he had earned one. The man was a common criminal and an agent who had failed. He'd been living with Mary Francom who in turn had been Robert's agent. She'd taken him for a ride at that, she'd made him look a fool. Yet he was worrying about her openly, staying on in Sestriere, babbling about his honour in his sweat-making foreign way, hinting at private motive, obligations. . . .

Major Mortimer snorted.

CHAPTER XV

Victor's plan had had a precise simplicity which he would have approved in the proposals of a subordinate. He had left Sestriere for a variety of reasons all of which seemed good to him, but he intended to return on Friday.

He had told the second porter at the Vallata, his face expressionless, that unexpected family business was obliging him to leave much earlier than he had intended. He wanted his bill and he wanted a car. Yes, he'd go down through the Montgenèvre to Briançon and there he would hire again. He'd pay the night rate without question. And it was all very urgent.

In his bedroom he packed with the speed of experience. This was a break indeed. He laughed aloud. They had handed it up on a platter.

And there had been other problems too—all solved. He knew he was being watched, and if he'd been in Maraldi's place he wouldn't have left it at watching. Maraldi would be trying to get rid of him, reporting to Turin, to Rome perhaps. In a day or two, when the administrative penny dropped, there would be a polite little visit from the *carabinieri*. Some irregularity in his papers. . . .

They'd escort him to the frontier.

All right, he'd beat them to it. He could do nothing till Friday evening, and time spent in Sestriere could be dangerous time. The heat was on him so he'd take it off. That was sound in principle and in this case it paid him twice. For he knew what Maraldi would think. Maraldi would quietly preen himself. . . . The formidable Victor had conceded best. He had come to Sestriere with God knew what foolish plan; had seen that it was stacked against him; left.

Maraldi would relax and that was fine.

Victor telephoned to the desk, and the second porter came up himself. Victor told him to shut the door and began to talk quickly. His instructions were precise. The porter was to contact a man in the transformer station and he wasn't to be seen doing so. The man was an Italian now, but there was an extraditable offence still. He'd do as he was told all right. So at any moment after seven-fifteen on the evening of Friday next. . . .

Understood?

The porter had understood; he had thought it absurd but he had understood. And he had information of his own which he had decided he wouldn't now pass. He had a brother in the telephone exchange and the families lived together. His brother was a chatterer, and a very important official in Rome had been telephoning to a Signor Maraldi at the Conte—special line, special clearance. It seemed that there was a wealthy foreigner at the Vallata, and later this evening the *carabinieri*. . . .

The porter had shut him up. The Vallata was full of foreigners. All of them were rich, and it wasn't extraordinary if one of them was of interest to some senior Roman official. This was 1963, and some very odd people had money. In any case he didn't want details. He wanted to keep his job.

He wanted to keep both of them and he didn't want trouble in either. Victor had had a tip-off, so why tell him something he knew already? The porter took Victor's bag down, putting it in the waiting car. He accepted his tip and went back to his desk. He was pleased to see Victor's back. He was a conscientious hotel servant as well as a minor agent, and he wanted no embarrassment for the more important of his employers. Victor was a potential liability; Victor could land him in serious trouble. But his money was useful, and it would certainly be stopped if he failed to deliver an urgent message. Very well then, he'd deliver it.

The porter shrugged. The message was crazy anyway.

In the car Victor lit a black cheroot. He knew what Maraldi would think. . . . Poor Victor, he was getting old; he wasn't the man he was, he'd had it really. Coming to Sestriere, looking around, seeing he could do nothing, slinking away with his tail down. . . .

The car slid down the mountain road and Victor smoked contentedly. At seven-fifteen next Friday. Rex Hadley had fixed it precisely. Rex Hadley and a woman—Hadley's woman.

Victor would be there—at ten minutes past seven; ten minutes past seven for seven-fifteen precisely. It shouldn't be impossible at all, indeed an occasional optimism worried him, for a lifetime of experience had taught him that in the byways of violence it was what looked easy which so often failed. That was sometimes bad luck, but the art of his profession was to eliminate the chances.

Victor had done everything possible towards that end. He knew that he was a marked man, but in a sense that was an advantage. A marked man was, by definition, marked by *something*: remove the something and it was unlikely that people would look too closely for the minor identifications which would have been circulated to them when a man lacked major. Victor's major identifications were one arm, grey hair cut *en brosse* and a characteristically solid peasant figure. He could do nothing about the last, but it wasn't decisive; plenty of men had powerful square figures. The first two he could change.

He had told the truth to the Vallata's porter, for at Briançon he had hired another car, driving fast through the rest of the night, arriving at his headquarters a little before lunchtime next day. He had been received with consideration and with authority unimpaired. Victor had smiled sardonically. The tall man was a mystic but he wasn't a fool.

There had been an immediate burst of action and a notable absence of questions, since Victor wasn't a man who took kindly to questions from his juniors. And the action had been effective. There hadn't been time to grow his hair long, but Victor's close-cropped grey was now jet black, his jet black eyebrows a frosty grey. The simple swap was startling. He decided that his mother wouldn't have known him, smiling again grimly, remembering that she seldom had.

The arm had been more difficult, but Victor hadn't asked the impossible. What was important was to let his pinned-up sleeve down, somehow to fill it. He could always wear gloves, and in the bitter winter of North Italy it would be natural to do so. He had an inch or two of arm below the shoulder still, and the rest which they brought him was very well made. It was useless to work with (or fight, he thought privately) but he could move it a little and not too unnaturally. He tried it now before a looking-glass. Not challenged to use it, keeping one hand in a pocket as this distinguished-looking stranger was entitled to do, it had an excellent chance of not being noticed. It wouldn't help driving a car, and now he must drive alone. But that didn't worry Victor. He could drive a car with one arm better than most men with two.

On Friday at noon he caught a plane to Turin. His passport said that he was Maître de Vence, the photograph supported it. For a moment he had been sourly amused. A lawyer and a de to his name at that. . . .

He was going up in the world.

They had arranged a hired car for him and it had met him at the airport. There had been a tricky moment as he had taken it over—a paper to sign on delivery and the fear that the driver might ask a lift back into the town. Victor didn't want it noticed that he drove one-handed. But the driver had been indifferent. Victor, one hand elegantly in his pocket still, had tipped him generously and asked for the car keys; then he had said that he was going back to the bar for a drink. The driver had agreed at once.

When Victor came back he had gone.

Now he was driving the Seicento deliberately, for he had looked at his watch. He had plenty of time, and to arrive in Sestriere too early would unnecessarily increase the risk of recognition. His plan was to arrive at ten past seven exactly and to leave his car in the square by the ski club. Then he would walk into it, turn left for the Banchetta cableway. . . .

If he ever got there.

Victor frowned, annoyed with himself. Of course he was going to get there. All the odds were that the check-points had been taken off, and if by some misfortune they had not, if he were challenged and Maître de Vence somehow recognized, then Maître de Vence was also Victor. He'd shoot if he had to, but as a final gambler's throw. And Victor detested gambling—all his instincts were to shorten the betting. For of course they'd shoot back and they'd be three or four to one. And they could telephone up the road, blocking it where they chose to and with disciplined and forewarned men. Victor's frown lifted slowly. He was here, was he not? and that was nine-tenths of it. At the airport nobody had given him a glance. His passport was a printed lie but they had stamped it without question; his bag was full of ski-ing clothes, for he was careful of detail. The Customs Officer had nodded approvingly, giving him a friendly smile, wishing him good sport. The snow, he had said, was splendid.

Victor drove on steadily, looking at his watch again, timing it. He even stopped for coffee.

At nine minutes past seven he parked his car outside the ski club. He took the keys but left the door open. That might be important though he didn't really think so. In the inevitable confusion there was a chance that he could reach his car again—say a hundred to one. Another hundred to one that he could make one of two frontiers in a Seicento before they caught him in a police car. Then a thousand to one that he could still get across it. A hundred by a hundred by a thousand. That was an accumulator of ten million to one. That wasn't one of Victor's bets.

It didn't matter. They'd take him of course and that would mean a lifer. But they couldn't prevent his consul talking to him, and the consul would send back again what Victor would tell him.

What Victor had come to get. From Hadley.

By the door of the ski club he paused. Within it was warm and light but outside almost dark. There was the hint of a moon, a presence still unrevealed. For a moment Victor looked back at the little car; then his shrug was as small. All that was irrelevant, an affair of ten million to one. It wasn't at bottom a part of his plan. Victor smiled almost happily for he had an advantage he recognized. He had sixty-four years and he wasn't ashamed of them. His own life didn't matter now, and when a man could say that and mean it a man could do almost anything.

Rex Hadley and Mary had walked down to the ski club. Rex was in very good spirits and Mary had caught them. The expedition intrigued her. Perhaps it was mildly foolish but it was undeniably romantic, and her life hadn't been so full of romance as to make her shudder at an occasional romanticism. Rex was as gay as a boy. Privately Mary doubted whether he could complete the run; he didn't ski really well yet—not well enough to guarantee the piste they intended—but she didn't mind that. At the worst they could walk down again, and there would still be the moon. Rex Hadley was happy and that was what mattered.

They were sitting in the cable-car waiting for it to start when the attendant came back to them. His manner was sheepish. A gentleman had arrived unexpectedly, asking if he might accompany them, a most distinguished signore. It seemed that the run to Banchetta by moonlight had certain associations for him. He would return in the car of course; he wouldn't interfere. If the lady and gentleman would be so kind. . . .

The attendant was sheepish but he had also been startled. Victor had startled him. He had recognized the voice at once but not the man. Victor had thought of that and hadn't fluffed it. He was a

very good judge of men and he had handled the attendant perfectly.
. . . The attendant was wondering who this stranger was, this
stranger with the familiar voice who had spoken of joining the
Englishman? But of course. And he hadn't yet fixed it with the
Englishman because he hadn't been able to. He had been away—his
wife had sent him. That explained everything, the white hair dyed,
the phoney arm (Victor had shifted it, smiling deprecatorily) the
general air of, well. . . .

Victor's manner had changed subtly. Now they were men, their
sex in common against another. Victor had done it beautifully.
They were men in their sixties and the attendant would be married.
Yes? Then his wife would be fifty, and at something past fifty the
sanest women. . . . Victor's smile had been an equal's, an equal con-
spirator's. It was extraordinary, he had said. You thought all that
nonsense was over, and suddenly—suddenly they had you dying
your hair and eyebrows, buying yourself false arms when for twenty
years they hadn't noticed that you lacked one. Still, you had to live
with them. The phase was tiresome but it passed. One *made* it pass.
Once, many years ago, he had gone up Banchetta by moonlight.
With his wife. There hadn't then been a cable-car but there had
been a moon. So one recaptured a mood perhaps, one did one's
duty. The same wife now awaited him, and if the English couple
could be persuaded to be obliging. . . .

The attendant had been flattered—Victor had intended it. He
said none of all this to Rex and Mary: instead he repeated that a
distinguished gentleman, a banker, he thought, perhaps a diplomat. . . .

Mary looked at Rex. For a moment he hesitated, but finally he
nodded. The attendant went away.

Almost at once Victor walked on to the platform. At the door of
the car he stopped, bowing with formality, saying in excellent
English: 'This is really very kind of you.'

'A pleasure.'

Victor sat down and the car began to move. They swung across the nursery slopes, six hundred yards without much climb, but at the foot of the mountain the cabin lifted sharply against the rise. An unexpected gulley opened below them and at once they seemed very high. The moon was behind the mountains still, its light in the plains but its reflection in the mountain sky. Victor rose quickly. 'I wish we could see more.'

'You will in a minute.'

Victor walked to the side of the car, staring at the lights below them. In the frosty air they shivered delicately. Incomprehensibly he pulled a torch out, flashing it on and off. To Rex it seemed senseless. In a minute there would be a moon, and at a hundred and sixty feet a torch was useless. He walked to the window by Victor, puzzled.

Suddenly there was an orange glare, an explosion half heard, half seen. Every light in the valley went out as one. The cable-car shuddered; ran on six feet on its own momentum; stopped. They swayed for an instant, then settled.

Both men sat down and the moon cleared the mountains. In the eerie light Victor said conversationally: 'That was the power-house. It's blown.'

Rex didn't answer—he was thinking. He had read about this. Some idiot French pilot had been fooling with a Mystère where he hadn't the right to be flying at all, and he'd smashed into a cableway. He'd cut the traction-cable and the cars had run back on the bearer. That had been bad enough, but eighteen inches difference and he'd have cut the bearer itself. But neither had happened here. The power had failed and that was all, but there was an auxiliary diesel engine— Rex had noticed it—and they could wind them back on it. Or if that were too chancy at night, there was always the relief car. It ran on the bearer like the others but had its own third wire to pull it. The Banchetta cableway wasn't one of those antiquated affairs which the provident Swiss were rumoured to sell to the Italians when they became too dangerous for their own safe use; it was a modern, highly efficient piece of engineering. Above all it was safe: great trouble had been taken to make it so. Instinctively Rex looked upwards. All three cables were intact. He took Mary's hand, said quietly: 'They'll soon get us out.'

'I doubt it.' Unexpectedly it was Victor.

'Why? If it's only a power failure.'

Victor said again: 'I doubt it.'

Rex Hadley was annoyed. 'Of course they will. They could wind us back on the second motor or more likely they'll put on the relief car and get us out in that. It hangs down a good way and you drop into it from the door at the back of this one.' Rex nodded across the cabin. 'It's a pretty small contraption but it's perfectly adequate. You'll have seen it in any case. They keep it hanging on the platform.'

'I've seen it—yes.'

'Then they'll have us out in no time.'

'No.'

'You mean they won't try?'

'I didn't say that.'

Rex shrugged irritably, settling to silence, lighting a cigarette and Mary's. In the frigid moonlight her face was calm. Presently he looked at his watch. Twenty minutes he had given them and ten had gone. He mustn't be impatient.

The car moved almost imperceptibly as a weight came on the bearer-wire. Victor rose. He walked to the back of the cabin, letting down the window, looking out. Rex Hadley joined him. Victor said impersonally: 'You were right—as far as you went. They've put on the relief car.'

Rex stared into the moonlight but he couldn't see a thing. He was thinking that Victor had remarkable eyesight. 'You're sure?'

'I am. I have very good sight still though I'm sixty-four.' The voice changed unexpectedly. 'I've often found that eyesight goes with general health. I should warn you that my own is excellent.'

Rex didn't answer since he hadn't one. . . . 'Tell you', 'warn you' —why warn? This elderly but powerful stranger spoke much too good English for an unintentional mistake in emphasis. Warn. . . .

Rex shrugged, staring again into the moonlight. He could see that the third wire was moving, and presently he picked up the relief car. It was climbing deliberately, not risking a jamb or too heavy a load on the auxiliary motor. Rex watched it with anxiety, telling himself he hadn't a reason. He found he had shivered but not with fear. Soon it would be very cold.

'Shouldn't we shut this window?'

'No.'

Rex looked once more at the open relief car. Two men were standing up in it, holding the arm from which it hung. One seemed to be the attendant and, as the car came nearer, Rex recognized the other. It was a man he had met. It was Robert Mortimer. Now why in the world should Robert Mortimer. . . ?

Suddenly he was sprawling, holding his plexus where Victor's blow had caught him. He hadn't even seen him move. But now Victor had turned and the gun was rock-steady. 'Don't move,' he said. 'Either of you. I must show you my back again but I warn you not to risk it. I can turn very quickly and my hearing's good too.'

He swung, firing from the open window, completing his turn in a single smooth movement. The gun had come back on Mary.

In the relief car there was instant silence. Robert said 'Victor' and the attendant picked up a walkie-talkie. He looked up inquiringly but Robert shook his head. The attendant's description of the other man in the cable-car had been that he was a well-built, middle-aged foreigner with black hair cut *en brosse*. Black hair, he had added, that had once been grey. Now, under gunfire, Robert's last doubt had gone.

The relief car had moved on five yards and in the cabin Victor heard it. He swung again and there was another flash. The attendant staggered but Robert caught him. He picked up the walkie-talkie and barked at it furiously. A single word.

The relief car stopped and Robert began to shout. 'Victor, we know it's you.' Swinging on a single wire in coolly ironical moonlight, Robert was aware of the banality. He tried again.

'Come off it, man. Be sensible. You haven't a hope in hell.'

Victor didn't answer him.

The relief car began to move again, but backwards. Very slowly it retreated and again Victor heard it. For an instant he turned his head but not the gun. Then he looked back at Rex and Mary.

'Now,' he said grimly.

CHAPTER XVI

Recollecting his emotions later, in the tranquillity which was supposed to be art but wasn't, Rex was grateful that at least Victor had spared them histrionics. The temptations of a certain melodrama must have been considerable, and a lesser man might easily have indulged them. But Victor had not. As the relief car slid away again he spoke with a brutal directness. 'My name doesn't matter, nor my job.' He looked at Rex Hadley but the pistol was still on Mary. 'Yours does. You're the head man at Maldington and Maldington *has* something. An American called Danziger has flown across to talk of it. I want it too and I mean to get it.'

Rex didn't reply. He had picked himself off the floor and Victor, not moving his pistol hand, had nodded at one of the benches. Rex Hadley sat down. For one thing he hadn't his breath back and for another he needed to think. The situation had a clarity which one part of his mind approved. According to Robert Mortimer there was the head of a foreign state who would give his eyes for an equal knowledge of Project A, and his agents had already tried twice. On both occasions Rex had himself been their target. The first attempt he hadn't known about till Mortimer had told him, and the second —well, the second had undeniably shaken him. But though it had shaken it had also prepared him. This powerful-looking stranger with the formidable in-fighting and the steady gun would be yet another agent of the same head of state. Rex was glad that he wasn't surprised since he knew that if he had been he would also have been frightened.

But though he wasn't frightened yet he didn't know what to do. He had fought in a war and he had recently and forcibly been reminded of it. But he knew nothing of man-to-man fighting, nothing of pistols and of the tricks which he had read could sometimes neutralize them. Sometimes, though, and with great good luck, for nobody pretended that a man with a pistol who knew how to use it hadn't an advantage against even an expert at unarmed combat. And Rex wasn't an expert at all; he couldn't even assess the risks. The cabin was very small (for all he knew that might weigh against the pistol-man) and there was an uncovenanted complication. The pistol was on Mary not himself. What did the expert do when the gun was on another man, a woman, Mary. . . ?

But Victor was talking again, laconic and menacing. 'I want it,' he repeated. 'The secret. And I'm going to have it.'

The cool moonlight in the little car was shattered by a searchlight. It was suddenly as bright as day. Victor laughed shortly. 'That will be Maraldi. Much good may it do him.' He was entirely confident.

And, Rex decided, rightly. The sides of the cabin, below the glass windows, were steel, but they wouldn't shoot through them in any case, not more than half blindly. And for a shot through the window the angle was hopeless . . . or was it? he wondered. Victor was standing, and for a very good shot the top of his head. . . . Just possibly. . . .

But Victor had seen it too, sat down again. He sat on the single seat, Mary to the left of him, Rex to the right. 'Tell,' he said dourly. 'Tell.'

Rex lit a cigarette. Now he was frightened but he was also pleased. His hand hadn't shaken or not very much.

'But that was cheap, but that was foolish. If you think you can bluff me——'

Victor had begun to snarl. He switched the gun at Rex's stomach.

Mary said softly: 'Hold, Rex, Hold.'

'Hold! You impertinent fool.' Victor was blazing now. 'You *amateur*.' It was the worst word he knew.

He flicked the gun back at Mary.

From the gulley below there was a sharp report. Rex waited for the bullet's whine but never heard it. Instead something snaked past the window, falling across the bearer wire, over the cabin but outside it. When it had settled Rex saw it was a rope.

Victor laughed contemptuously. 'Rocket escape-line—useless. You could reach that rope and pull on it. Up would come a bigger one, a rope ladder perhaps. You could get down if you had the nerve, or another man could climb up. Another armed man. All this could happen if you could reach that line. You won't, of course. We're quite alone—we'll stay so.' Victor was talking calmly now. His sudden rage was spent.

Rex looked at him. He much preferred him angry. Now he was master and knew it, talking again smoothly: 'I don't care how tough you think you are, how many cigarettes you smoke. I've broken brave men and I'd break you too. In time, that is—directly. But I needn't waste time, I'm not obliged to. This woman here. . .'

He looked from Rex to Mary. The gun was already on her. She said something in French.

There was a single shot.

For a moment Rex didn't register. Mary was bending down. She had taken a foolish handkerchief from an even more frivolous bag; she was tying her leg up silently. Rex watched her in a sort of dream, half seeing her. What he saw was a handkerchief, red.

He rushed Victor by instinct, swinging absurdly, and in an instant he was flat again. He staggered across the little car, crashing against the opposite side, smashing the glass and falling. He hadn't been shot but he wished he had. His hands were between his legs, holding his crutch helplessly. Enormous waves of agony came up at him, black ones, then scarlet. He couldn't breathe and he couldn't move. He wished he could die but knew he mustn't. He fought for his life.

Victor was standing over him but the pistol was still on Mary. She hadn't moved nor spoken again. Victor's face was a stone. 'Talk,' he said wickedly. 'Talk for your lady love.'

Francis de Fleury had passed three days in an increasing awareness of futility. It had been one thing to keep close to Victor, something which could be done quite openly since Victor himself was being watched by professionals and could hardly complain to them that a freelance had cut in; but Rex Hadley and Mary were much more difficult, not amateur's work at all. He hadn't been trained in shadowing and they'd spot him at once. They wouldn't go to the police, they'd simply challenge him. . . . What in hell did he think he was playing at?

de Fleury sighed. Besides, he thought, he would be watching blind. For what? For Victor's return? He considered it unlikely, since he could think of nothing which couldn't equally well be carried out by one of Victor's men. And probably better. Victor had been here to scout, not act. So de Fleury would be watching for someone he didn't know, some plan he hadn't an inkling of. Instinct insisted that there would be further violence, and de Fleury respected instinct; but reason told him coolly that he himself was useless. Only his pride had kept him in Sestriere. He had told Robert Mortimer he intended to stay and that was an undertaking.

Which was something one stood by.

On Friday evening he had been drinking an aperitif when all the lights went out. It didn't strike him as significant—power lines did fail. especially mountain ones—but he had been irritated. They had been slow with the candles in the bar, and presently he saw that there were lights again in the ski club. Probably they had batteries. He left money on the table and walked idly across the square. He pushed the door open.

At once he knew that something had happened. An attendant was talking to an increasing crowd of tourists. There was a car up there—stuck. Of course it was quite all right. Three people on a special trip but they'd get them down in no time. They had put on the relief car and the engineer was starting up the diesel. There was nothing to worry about, nothing at all. Routine.

Suddenly the hall was full of police. Their plain-clothes leader cut through the crowd, straight to the attendant.

. . . Three people in the car up there? What people?

An Englishman and his wife.

Staying at the Conte?

Yes.

A second's silence.

And the third person with them?

An elderly man, a foreigner.

Describe.

Sixty to sixty-five. Thickset and powerful. He had been here before but had left and returned. He'd altered his appearance, dyed his hair. . . .

There was an oath but a further question. Then where had the car stuck?

Just at the bottom, above that gulley.

Another oath but instant action. Maraldi swung on the policemen. . . . The searchlight, the rocket-gear. Run.

They ran.

de Fleury saw that Robert Mortimer had joined Maraldi. He slipped quietly across to them, listening. Maraldi was saying savagely: 'He's got them alone—the two of them. Victor himself. They're up in that stalled cable-car.'

'You're certain it's Victor?'

'Morally.'

Robert said softly: 'Is that a fact?'

'You don't seem to understand me. If it's Victor himself——'

'I understand you perfectly. So how do we bring them down?'

170

'They're putting on the rescue car.'

'I'll go in it then.'

'*I'll* go.'

Robert said patiently: 'Think. I heard you giving orders and there's plenty to do down here still. You're head man here and I don't count. We don't want a panic and we don't want the Press. You cut the ice, I don't.'

'Mother of God, I——'

'Get this mob out of here. Go down to the gulley with the searchlight. Try the escape-line, though it doesn't sound hopeful. Take charge. Use your loaf.'

Maraldi hesitated and Robert pushed him gently. At last he shrugged and turned.

The police began to clear the hall, but de Fleury touched Robert Mortimer. 'Hullo.'

'Oh, hullo.'

'I've been eavesdropping.'

'Yes, I saw you.'

'I'd like to go along with you.'

'But why?'

'I told you that once.'

'You're a very strange sort of blackmailer.'

de Fleury said furiously: 'People are always telling me I'm strange. I simply don't see it. Mary Francom is up there, with Victor——'

'I'm afraid there won't be room for you.'

'But——'

Robert looked deliberately at the two *carabinieri* still in the hall. 'But you can stay here,' he said. 'I'll tell them.'

He did so, turning, walking out to the platform and the waiting relief car. de Fleury began to pace the hall—eight strides, a turn, and eight again. He was lighting one cigarette from another.

Twenty minutes later Robert had come back again. He was supporting the attendant. 'Nothing too serious. A shot in the shoulder. Lucky.' One of the *carabinieri* led the attendant away, and Robert walked up to de Fleury. 'I suppose,' he said mildly, 'I suppose you can't lend me a gun? They're tying a sort of shield to the relief car—the top of the oil tank, I think it is—but it's better than nothing.' He looked at the remaining *carabiniere*. 'That bobby will have a pistol but it's not one I'm used to. Me, I never carry one but we all know you do. They frisked your room.' Unexpectedly his voice was almost wheedling. 'Now that nice little Colt of yours, or Luger. . . .'

Very slowly de Fleury put his hand in his pocket, and when it came out it was holding a gun. It was holding it by the barrel and Robert approved. He put his hand out to take the butt, smiling his thanks, and for a second he was off balance.

de Fleury knocked him cold.

The *carabiniere* began to move, but now the gun was pointed. 'Keep very still.'

de Fleury ran across the hall, out through the glass partition doors, on to the platform. In the control room the engineer could see nothing of the hall; all he saw from his window was that the shield had been lashed to the relief car and that a man had just jumped into it. An armed man who waved at him urgently. He pulled a lever and the relief car began to move.

Francis de Fleury let his breath out softly.

He sat down in the open box, behind the makeshift armour, coolly assessing his chances. They weren't, he decided, brilliant. The top of the oil tank, though only iron, would probably stop an ordinary pistol bullet, but he had nothing to fire through and the shield wasn't more than four feet high. The relief car itself hung well below the bearer-wire—a man being rescued dropped into it from the cable-car—and that meant that Victor would be shooting down at him. He was safe enough crouched behind his improvised gun-shield and provided he kept a respectful distance, but he didn't propose to spend a night crouched uselessly behind a gun-shield. He'd have to stand up to shoot, to kneel at best, and that meant exposing head, chest and shoulders. Whereas Victor, shooting down at him, would show him two eyes, a pistol hand at most at the cable-car's open window. And below it was solid steel.

Francis de Fleury smiled. And that wasn't all of it. The mountain weather, notoriously unpredictable, had turned against him. Now the moon was behind a sudden cloud; a cold wind blew in fickle gusts. The car had begun to swing—not dangerously, but it would be a very poor platform for a gun duel. The cable-car might be swinging too but, heavier, much less.

de Fleury looked at his gun. Guns were a hobby. This one, he remembered, was his second. Mary had taken the first—Mary in that cable-car with Victor.

He stood up without knowing it, staring into a sudden blur of snow. He had come perhaps half-way, and, as the flurry cleared, he could see the cable-car ahead of him. The searchlight lit it mercilessly. It hung on a single wire, a tiny world and quite alone, white in the searchlight's glare.

Another squall rocked the rescue car and de Fleury sat down. As he did so the walkie-talkie buzzed at him. He picked it up unthinkingly and a cool voice said crisply: 'Robert Mortimer here.'

'Don't stop the wire, I beg you. Please.'

There was an incomprehensible English laugh. 'My friend I wouldn't think of it. There isn't time to wind you in, and I'm in no shape to take your place.'

'I'm sorry about that, I——'

'Forget it. And good luck.'

The walkie-talkie went dead and de Fleury stood up again. He was sixty yards away by now, but the angle was against him, as were the cable-car's steel sides. Even standing he couldn't see into it. In any case he'd have to make Victor shoot at him. He couldn't just run up to them, try to climb in, to board them. That would be suicide. He'd have to fire first—draw fire. Victor wasn't a man to be shot at without answering. So one into the cabin first, through the open back window, upwards. And pray it wouldn't ricochet. The roof might be wood, or lined. . . .

He'd have to risk it.

He fired as a third squall struck him, squarely now. The shot went away, but uselessly, even the report lost in the screaming wind. The open car swung wildly and de Fleury fell to save himself. He felt sick but he was still quite calm. Swinging like this, a human pendulum, he wouldn't hit a haystack. And the car was running on still. Forty yards now, no, less. . . .

He picked up the walkie-talkie again. He told Mortimer to stop him.

When the rescue car stopped at last de Fleury peeped out of it. Now it was ten yards. The range had shortened but not the odds: on the contrary they had lengthened, and against him. He was much too close and much too low. Victor, when he shot at him, would be a fancy target indeed. And the shield was useless now.

Francis de Fleury laughed. He was a sitting duck and knew it. Well, at least he needn't fire again; he needn't waste bullets attracting attention.

He stood up yet again as the car for an instant steadied; he filled his lungs with icy air and shouted.

'Victor.'

Nothing.

'Victor, you bastard swine.'

There was the flicker of a target, eyes and a hand. de Fleury fired and the cruel wind jerked the rescue car. He knew he had missed but Victor hadn't. He'd been going for the body and he'd got it. de Fleury collapsed. He had dropped the gun but it had fallen under him.

. . . Victor wouldn't see it there, he'd think it had gone overboard. There was a chance he wouldn't shoot again. . . . A man in a little box, sprawled on his face, dead probably and anyhow disarmed. . . .

Victor was a peasant and he hated waste.

de Fleury lay very still. He was hit pretty badly but he wasn't dead.

When he was sure no second shot was coming he felt for the pistol and dragged himself to his knees. He was bleeding internally and very cold. He forced himself upright, groaning softly, holding the shield for support, focusing the cable-car through mists of pain. He gave himself a minute more of consciousness—a minute and a half at most. Then he would be out for good.

In the lull in the wind he fired a third shot at nothing. At that range it must be heard.

In the cable-car Victor had returned to Rex and Mary. Killing de Fleury hadn't given him a twinge. The man had always been a playboy, not worth a thought, and now it was certain he'd changed sides. The rat—he'd earned his bullet. But though de Fleury hadn't worried him Victor was worried. The affair wasn't developing as he had expected. Mary was sitting quietly—much too quietly to suit Victor. He had hoped for hysteria, for tears at least: her contemptuous silence shook him for it didn't suit his plan. With a shinbone smashed she hadn't uttered. She wasn't helping him at all, she wasn't playing. She might have been at her hairdresser's.

. . . All right, he'd show them. They thought they were tough, but he'd seen brave men and women pitiably broken. He himself had done the breaking. He raised the gun again, sighting at Mary's shoulder now, but lowered it. It would be premature to shoot again since Rex couldn't speak yet. He'd keep that for when he could—for when it paid. He looked down at Rex Hadley, writhing, fighting for breath and more, his hands between his legs still, holding himself together. Time, Victor remembered suddenly, was running against him. Sooner or later they'd manage to pull the car down.

A lifetime's discipline cracked in insane frustration. To plan and to come so close; to offer his own freedom up, the rest of his life in prison. He almost wept. The fools, the unaccountably stubborn fools. This grovelling thing on the floor, this crippled Englishman. . . .

Victor balanced himself carefully, raising his right foot. He was aiming at Rex's hands. It would kill him of course, so he'd never talk.

For an appalling instant it didn't matter. Victor swung his foot once slowly, measuring the final blow. His face was a mask of hate.

Deliberately he dropped his knee again. Outside the cable-car he'd heard a shot.

It sobered him at once. This was another interruption, something to be attended to, and finally. He turned his back on Rex and Mary for he didn't fear either: he turned his back but he also bent it. On this side of the car no bullet could reach him, but as he moved across it to the window. . . . A target perhaps, a second's target.

He slipped across the cable-car bent double, checking his gun as he went, and behind the steel below the window he collected himself. . . . Up for an instant, sight and shoot. He'd finish it this time, he couldn't miss.

He heard movement behind him and turned his head, incredulous. Rex Hadley was coming after him. If that was what you called it. He was dragging himself by his elbows, his legs hanging uselessly behind him, like a reptile, Victor thought unexpectedly, the lowest of creation. He watched in fascination. Rex was gasping, in evident agony. . . . Heave on an elbow, gasp, and wait. His face shone with sweat. Another heave, another bitter foot, and wait again. Only his eyes were steady and they never left Victor's.

Victor raised his gun but dropped it. He was sane again now. Killing Hadley would be fatal. He put the gun back in his pocket.

He waited impassively as Rex inched towards him. Then he bent down a little more, grasping his coat collar. He had only one arm but it was very strong. He pulled Rex to his knees and somehow he stayed there. Rex struck weakly at Victor's belly, an overarm swing, feeble and in any case outranged. Victor ignored it. He drew back his own good arm, instinctively straightening.

The blow never fell. Victor dropped inexplicably, down on Rex Hadley, knocking him off his knees again. Rex lay quite still, grimly awaiting further punishment. None came. When Victor didn't move again Rex pulled himself back on his elbows. It was the last of his strength. Victor lay motionless. He was lying on his face and he was dead. There was a neat small hole in the back of his head and Rex didn't try to turn it.

Somehow he found breath once more. 'Mary. . . the rescue line . . . pull it in.'

Through a blur of receding consciousness he saw that she had heard him. She had risen on her single leg, steadying herself against the cable-car's sides. She hobbled to the window his first fall had shattered and at last reached the line. She began to pull it in. There seemed to be a mile of it but finally a rope came up—two ropes, a ladder. Mary made it fast and Rex saw it tauten.

'There's a man climbing up.'

Rex didn't hear her.

CHAPTER XVII

In Colonel Russell's room in the Security Executive Sir William Banner was talking, and Russell, who was good at it, was listening. Banner was saying: 'J. Wallis Danziger—you'll have heard of him, of course.'

'Of course. And I know that he's over here. What's more I know he came to see you.'

'You're interest doesn't surprise me, but I doubt if you bugged my house. So I've come to tell you what we settled.'

'Kind of you,' Russell said.

'Not kind. I avoid unnecessary trouble when I can—trouble for you and embarrassment for myself.' Sir Bill slid away at an apparent tangent. 'Americans,' he said. 'I like them.'

'Yes?'

'Or rather I respect them. The orthodox attitude about America seems to be a sort of jealous sneer. I can understand the jealousy—there are psychological reasons though I won't bore you by deep-down-delving—but the sneer annoys me. I think it's ungrateful. If it weren't for America Europe would be one big Satellite, and that includes this country. I know they drink nasty beverages and their breakfasts don't agree with me; they're even unenlightened enough to believe that competition works, and there are circles where that's worse than original sin. The certainty remains that their power protects us. It isn't a position I relish but it's a political fact.'

'So you've taken them in on Project A? You felt you owed them a share of it?'

Sir William clucked impatiently. 'I didn't say that at all. That savours of moral judgement, which is something I much mistrust. You know what we've been trying for at Maldington—the most powerful conventional explosive known. And I see it as an ugly race. Sooner or later somebody is going to succeed, and I'd rather go in with friends than risk an enemy getting there ahead of us.'

'Why shouldn't we get there alone?'

'Because we can't. We're as near to the thing in theory as we'll ever be, but there's a gap between a scientists' theories and established production. In this case that's a gap of sheer resources. We simply don't have them and Danziger does.'

Russell stroked his chin. 'I don't say I disagree with you—I don't know enough to dare to. But what will the politicians say?'

'What *can* they say? Our masters have just two choices which make sense: they could shut down Maldington, cutting their losses, or they could commit say a hundred million more to a programme where there's still no absolute certainty of final success. They won't do the latter—we can't afford it—and they won't cut their losses because it isn't in their nature to. There would be too many questions and no easy answer—that's what they go for, the easy answer. Any government disintegrating does. So they'd just keep us on at half-cock. I'm a European before I'm any sort of a party man, and I don't think that's good enough.'

'So the whole thing goes over to America? Danziger takes the lot?'

'Good heavens, no. Rudi Walther is what he really wants. I've sounded him and he feels as I do. So Walther will go but Maldington stays. There'll be plenty of work which can perfectly well be done there. In some ways better—Danziger admits it.'

'And what about the other scientists?'

'Well, *what* about them? I don't employ them directly, and I suppose the Ministry could withdraw them if it wanted to. But I don't think it will. What's the use of an empty establishment? In any case, second-flight scientists are nine for sixpence—I could always go out and hire others. But none of that will happen, I assure you. I've been careful about Maldington—tactful.' Sir William smiled ironically. 'Besides, I've a social conscience. Call Maldington my bow at full employment.'

Russell made a surprising sound.

'You don't have to believe me. What I can prove is my tenancy at Maldington. That has six months to run still.'

With a rare hint of malice Charles Russell said: 'You seem to have fixed it beautifully.'

'I'm glad you approve.'

But Russell had recovered his good humour. Sir William Banner was an arbitrary man, but he had virtues which in a tycoon were most unusual. Moreover it would be a very bold layman who said he had chosen wrongly. Russell wasn't one of them and only time would tell. He asked now quietly, as bland as milk: 'You'll leave Hadley in charge at Maldington?'

'Who better? How is he, by the way?'

'I rang this morning and the news is good. He'll be out in a day or two and they assure me there's nothing permanent. Nothing which need disturb a married man.'

'That's very good.'

'It's a very good hospital.'

'de Fleury's in it too, I think. He'll live?'

'He will.'

'That's a very brave scoundrel. We owe him plenty.'

'I think so too. And when he comes out of hospital he can hardly go back to his own country, or not for a bit at any rate. He'll need money and we've thought of that. Just between the two of us we've done rather more than think. There'll be something waiting for him when he's finally discharged.'

'If I may ask—how much?'

Charles Russell told him.

'I'd like to double that.'

'You're really very generous.'

'Perhaps.' Sir William shrugged. 'And that reminds me—I owe you lunch. Come on.'

In his overheated room the tall man was reading a report and frowning. . . . Those intolerable Anglo-Saxons. So the Americans had bought themselves in and he knew what that meant. It meant that his hopes of Project A had gone. America was a long way away, and American security would be grimly on notice. Opinions varied whether it was better than British: some said it was and some that it wasn't. The fact remained that it was much less hamstrung by the rule of law. Like Sir William Banner the Marshal had a great respect for the Americans.

But no love at all.

He turned to another paper for he had a problem more pressing. He had lost Project A but the Fourteenth Bureau had other tasks, and a successor to Victor was essential. The obvious heir apparent was this Reynard. He'd seen long service as Victor's assistant and the Army was pressing his claims. But the tall man shook his head. This Reynard had family, perhaps a little money still, and those meant an independence, even a mind of one's own. Which wouldn't suit the Marshal. Whereas there was this other man, born in the provinces of modest stock, fighting his own way upwards. Another Victor. Appoint him and you appointed a dependant.

For an instant the Marshal thought of Victor. But not for a long one. Victor was dead; Victor had been expendable.

He picked up the paper and wrote a name. Then he poured half a glass of wine, for he was frugal. He decided he'd been intelligent.

It was a decision he took more frequently as senility stalked him.

In a fine modern hospital in Turin Mary was being wheeled into

Rex's room. She was in plaster still but cheerful. They chatted of nothing till the nurse went out, then Rex said happily: 'There've been changes—Sir William telephoned. But they're leaving me at Maldington.'

'I'm glad of that. I've been pushed around plenty, country to country. I didn't want to change again.'

'You'll like it in England? Always?'

'Buy me a grave there.'

'Talking of graves,' he said, 'they're burying Victor tomorrow. Here.'

'Aren't they sending back the body?'

'No. He hadn't kith or kin, you see, and they wouldn't dare ask for him officially.' There was a reflective English silence, then: 'I think I'll send some flowers,' he said.

She stared at him, unbelieving. 'I'll never understand you, Rex.'

'Then we're going to be very happy.'